Praise for Term

Brilliant and tir
Alan Steele-Nic. ... . US senator
Jacob Javits

Required reading before November election.
Patrick Carswell, Amazon reviewer

Mr. Powell is one h*** of a storyteller.
D. W. Hawk, Amazon reviewer

A real page turner, this psychological thriller holds many truths – both spoken and unspoken – about America's current political problems. Term Limits is dark, violent, but also very passionate about how political corruption damages the live of ordinary Americans. This novel could be required reading for all readers no matter what their political views.
Amazon Review

Steve Powell has walked a literary tightrope that skillfully balances him between a fast paced whodunit and a concise, well reasoned political dissertation on term limits. As a thriller, the plot will pull you into a rollercoaster ride with twists and turns that will keep you turning pages long into the night. As a political OpEd, the book persuasively and poignantly argues for term limits in a way that should cause both Democrats and Republicans to finally agree on something. Powell does all of this while bringing us into the heart and mind of the killer. Fun, thought provoking and scary, all at the same time. 5 Stars.
Amazon Review

CLARET PRESS

Copyright ©Steve Powell, 2025
The moral right of the author has been asserted.

Cover and Interior Design by Petya Tsankova

ISBN paperback: 978-1-910461-86-0
ISBN ebook: 978-1-910461-87-7

A CIP catalogue record for this book is available from the British Library.

www.claretpress.com

stupid

Chapter 1:

The harbor wasn't busy, but there was activity. People were scattered over the dozen or so docks, cleaning and securing boats, drinking, partying and eating late suppers. Some were still plodding their way in from the lake. I felt safe.

I made my way down the last dock, to the spot where we were supposed to meet. I purposefully scanned each boat and tried to make eye contact with everyone I saw. No one seemed to be waiting for me.

Near the end of the dock, I stopped and looked south toward Chicago's skyline. I checked the nearest docks. No one appeared to be watching me. I looked east across the water. Lakeshore Drive, which ran between the harbor and Lake Michigan, was at a standstill with bumper-to-bumper traffic in both directions.

It was almost dusk. A boat emerged from an underpass, puttering in towards the docks. There didn't seem to be anyone driving or even on board.

Then a head popped up.

I saw a flash. And another. Something pierced my chest. Then my neck. Gunshots.

The impact pushed me back and to my right. My hands moved to the pain. My legs tangled and gave way. I stumbled and fell face first into the lake.

Chapter 2:

My name is Philip Osgood. I'm a bond trader. For the past twenty-five years I've run a small hedge fund in Greenwich, Connecticut. The same year I opened the fund I met the man responsible for me being shot. His name was Emile Coulon.

That was back in 1994. I was thirty-four. That year I'd decided to leave the bank I was working for on Wall Street and start my own fund. It was a risky move, but one I never regretted. The day I met Emile I was moving into my first office since branching off on my own. The office was an interior, glass-fronted room on the first floor of a modern, six-story building in Greenwich, next to the train station. It was a far cry from my corner seat on a massive trading floor on the 48th floor of a skyscraper on Manhattan's southern tip, overlooking the Statue of Liberty, but it suited my needs.

I met Emile on a Saturday. I was setting up the ten-by-twelve-foot room. The furniture, an L-shaped desk, a credenza and three chairs, had been delivered the day before. My task that Saturday was to place and secure a small satellite dish on the building's roof, then connect a cable to the dish, drop the cable through a pre-existing conduit, down six stories to the ceiling level of the first floor, snake it above the ceiling panels in the hallway of the first floor to my office, to the wall beside my desk, down through the wall to a hole near the floor and finally to connect the cable to my computer.

When you worked for a money center bank in New York, especially in the 1980s and '90s, if you wanted a new computer or phone bank or almost anything else, the "tech guys" took care of it. This was all new to me. But to be honest it was all pretty simple and kind of fun.

Once the satellite was secured on the roof and the cable was dropped and connected to my computer, things got a little trickier. To monitor the markets I traded, I could lease a Bloomberg terminal like the one I'd used at the bank, for $1800 a month, or use a satellite feed to get quotes directly from the exchanges on which I traded, for $125 a month. I went for the $125 satellite option.

I was told I could save another $250 by installing the satellite myself. I was skeptical, but the man on the phone representing the company that provided the feed assured me that the process wasn't too difficult. While he built my confidence, my wife Jenny, who could only hear my half of the conversation, looked less than certain. Still, I enlisted her help and she gamely worked with me.

Jenny's contribution began after the cable dropping was done. When she arrived, I was sitting behind my modest desk, sweaty and soiled, reading an instruction manual. I'm not sure she saw Gordon Gekko when she looked at me, but she kept her thoughts to herself. I explained that her role would be to sit at my desk and stare at the computer screen, to which I'd connected the cable from the satellite dish that I hoped was still on the roof. She was to watch the screen and let me know if I acquired a signal. She rightly asked how I intended to find that particular signal in all of outer space. Ever the naïve optimist I proudly showed her the tools that had come in my satellite installation kit: a cheap-looking plastic compass, an even cheaper-looking azimuth and a few Allen wrenches. At that point we'd only been married for nine years, but she was already pretty good at knowing when I was in over my head. She gave me a familiar look.

I considered explaining that the azimuth would help me to point the dish in the direction of the celestial object, in this case my satellite, expressed as the angular distance from the north point of the horizon to the point at which a vertical circle passing through the object, my satellite, intersects the horizon, but I thought better of it. Instead, I took my cheap tools and my brand-new first cell phone and left for the roof. Truthfully, I didn't think there was a chance in hell I'd find the satellite, but anyone who has ever been married surely understands that I couldn't back down. I headed up.

Thirty minutes later my cell phone rang. It was Jenny.

"How's it going up there?"

"Fine. How are you?"

It was windy on the roof, but I heard a satisfied chuckle.

"Give me twenty more minutes. I think I've got this."

"Sure, honey."

I hung up and got back to work. Thirty or forty minutes later I called my office.

A lovely-sounding woman's voice answered the phone. "Hello. Hapless Investments. May I help you?"

I ignored her. "Have you seen the signal?"

She kindly responded, "Nothing yet."

"Okay. Stay on the line. I think I'm close."

I put the phone on speaker and laid it on the roof then looked at the three-foot dish, pointing into space. I reread the azimuth instructions and adjusted the dish slightly.

"Holy shit!"

"What?"

"There's a signal. You did it. You found the fucker!"

Jenny didn't often swear. She was in shock. I think I was even more surprised.

For the record, that signal held for three years, until a storm shifted my dish. Celestial navigator that I was, after the storm I went back to the roof and, again, found the signal.

At any rate on that first Saturday back in 1994, I gathered my tools and headed down to my sure-to-be impressed wife. All the way down I imagined my triumph. Would she kiss me? Look at me in awe? I tried to put on my most matter-of-fact, humble look as I stepped into my office.

Things never work out the way they're supposed to. She was talking to some guy.

I stepped in.

Jenny smiled. "Hello, Copernicus."

God but I loved her.

She teasingly ignored the lustful look in my eyes and said, "Phil, this is Emile Coulon. He has the offices across from yours."

Coulon smiled and extended his hand. "Hey Phil, nice to meet you. Jenny was just telling me that you actually found the satellite."

I liked him from the start.

Chapter 3:

For my first few years in Greenwich, I worked hard to attract clients and grow my fledgling fund. Consequently, I pretty much lived at the office and often had dinner there. The nature of Emile's business kept him in his office to all hours as well. He was a former cop who became a private detective. That's right, a private eye. I'd never met one before and I certainly didn't expect to find one in the offices next to mine in Greenwich-fucking-Connecticut. But Emile was there and compared to the other would-be masters of the universe in our building, he was a breath of fresh air.

After a few months of smelling each other's pizza or Chinese food, we started to occasionally order dinner together. While Emile had a tremendous gift for gab, he also knew when to shut up and let me work. I respected his space as well. Some nights we divvied up the food and went to our own offices, and other nights we ate together. Along the way, we became friends. When we did eat together, I routinely grilled him about his business. He was making a small fortune helping suspicious Greenwich husbands and wives keep tabs on their suspected, usually unsuspecting spouses. I found the work fascinating.

When we first met, Emile was about forty-five and twice divorced. He was a little guy, maybe 5'8" and 150 pounds. He had gleaming blue eyes and some silver hair surrounding a bald, tan scalp. And he had an infectious grin that made you want to spend time with him. He was smart as a whip and funny as could be. The first time anyone met him they had a sense he was going to be fun and, his two ex-wives notwithstanding, it was true.

After a few years of listening to his stories and after my business was fairly well established, I asked him to take me along on a case. He tried to dissuade me, but I nagged until he finally agreed.

I can still remember the case. A Greenwich woman in her early thirties was convinced that her forty-four-year-old, incredibly wealthy husband was cheating. She had good reason to be suspicious – she'd been his mistress for several years until she convinced him to leave his first wife for her. The husband, Howard Rawlings, ran a private equity fund in Larchmont, New York, a nice suburb north of the city. The fund had offices in a large complex with a huge outdoor parking area that served several buildings, so surveillance there was easy. On weekday mornings Emile would simply park in the lot near but not too close to the front entrance of Rawlings' building and wait. Rawlings typically got to work at 8:30. By that time the lots were almost full so it was easy for Emile to blend in.

As we sat waiting, I can still remember how excited I was.

Coulon laughed. "What do you think is going to happen here?"

"I'm not sure."

He looked at me, pretending to already regret bringing me along. Rather than explaining what was going to happen, he reached behind his seat and retrieved a bag from a coffee shop. Ever the ball-buster, he took out one steaming cup of coffee and a single lemon poppy muffin. I looked at him and then into the bag. It was empty.

"Seriously?"

"What? I'm supposed to buy you breakfast?"

I muttered to myself.

He sipped his coffee and ate his muffin.

"What kind of car does he drive? Do you think he'll be here soon?"

Emile took off his sunglasses and rubbed his eyes, exhausted by my enthusiasm.

"He usually drives a navy-blue Mercedes wagon or some-times a grey Audi A8."

He looked down at his watch. "He generally gets here be-tween 8:20 and 8:30, so keep your eyes peeled there, Kato."

In spite of the shit he was giving me, I did keep them peeled.

Five minutes later a navy-blue Mercedes wagon pulled in off the street and into our part of the lot. I watched silently. I wasn't going to give Emile the satisfaction of asking if it was Rawlings. We both watched as a tall, casually-but-well-dressed man in his forties stepped from the car, took a briefcase from the backseat and walked through the front door of the building.

Neither of us said a word. It was driving me nuts. I was pretty sure the man was Rawlings, but not positive. Dozens of cars pulled into the complex, including several Audi sedans, but none came into our building's lot.

After ten minutes Emile pulled the brim of his baseball cap down over the upper half of his face. He settled back and closed his eyes.

"What are you doing?"

"I'm going to take a nap."

"A nap?"

"Yeah. The tall guy was Rawlings. He'll probably be in there until lunch, unless he has an earlier meeting in the city. Let me know if he comes out."

I just grunted and settled back.

After a minute he said, "Do you want some coffee?"

I looked at him in disbelief. With the brim still pulled down he smiled and said, "There's a bag behind your seat. Help your-self."

"Asshole."

About seventy minutes later Emile woke up. Rightly con-fident that I'd been laser-focused he stretched and asked, "Any activity?"

"Not from our guy. What floor is his office on?"

Emile pointed to the top right-hand corner of the four-story suburban office building. "The top. His office is in that corner."

I looked up but couldn't see in. The sun was reflecting off the glass.

"How much do you get paid to do this?"

He just smiled.

"Seriously. How much?"

"$160 an hour plus expenses, more if I have to travel. $2500 minimum in the form of a non-refundable deposit."

"Seriously?"

He nodded again.

"All that money, just to follow him?"

"Yup."

"Do you ever actually have to do anything? Confront anyone?"

He smiled and took off the cap. "Sometimes."

"What sort of things?"

"It varies, but in a situation like this when I'm tracking a person who works, I sometimes need to get creative. It's not like he's going to fuck in the parking lot or in his family room, in a place where I can snap pictures. He'll be more cautious than that, especially this guy, since he's been through this before."

He gave me some background on Rawlings, explaining the first divorce and how a private investigator had countless pictures of him and his former mistress, now wife, in restaurants, hotel lobbies and even embracing and kissing on a beach in Bermuda.

I realized he was speaking from memory.

"You were the detective?"

"Yup."

"Doesn't Rawlings know you? Won't he recognize you?"

"I was worried about the same thing. But when his ex-mistress/current wife hired me, she said he doesn't know who I am. She said he never really cared about the detective who caught him cheating on his first wife. He didn't think it was the detective's fault, my fault. The guy's pragmatic. He took a calculated risk and it didn't pan out. Or maybe he didn't care if he got caught. His current wife Gina is sure that he has no idea who I was or am."

"So, what's the plan?"

"This is only my fourth day following him, but I'm starting to get a sense of his patterns. He usually works here for three or four hours until lunchtime. If he's heading into the city, he generally leaves between eleven and twelve. If he's staying out here, he either stays in the office all day or sometimes goes to his gym for an hour. The nice thing is, he seems to be vaguely honest with his wife about where he'll be during the day. He tells her and she tells me. She told me that today he's heading into the city for some meetings and then a client dinner."

"Have you seen him with anyone so far? Anyone suspicious?"

"No. On Tuesday he did go into the city and had a lunch, but it was with a bunch of suits. Then he went to a couple of meetings. They seemed legitimate. One was at Lehman and another at a smaller brokerage firm. I can't follow him into those buildings and certainly not into the firms, but so far he hasn't ditched me or done anything to try to make it hard to follow him."

"What do you mean?"

"Think about it. It's not like I'm the FBI with ten agents on a stakeout. Normally it's just me sitting in a car or walking around and hanging out near the front of a building he went into, waiting for him to come out."

"So, if he was suspicious and went out the back door, you'd never know."

"Exactly. And these office buildings are often half of a city block. If I stay on or near a corner, I can cover two sides, but that leaves two more. Even if he isn't sneaking around, if he goes in the east side of a building and his next meeting is west of the building, chances are he'll go out the west side and I'll lose him."

I smiled. "You need me."

He shook his head and laughed. "I'm doing just fine without you."

"Yeah but think how much easier it is with two of us. How many times have you sat in front of a building for hours after the person you're following has gone?"

"It happens."

"You need me."

"I need you today. If you weren't here, I'd have someone else with me. There are a few other guys I sometimes work with. We help each other from time to time."

Emile nodded toward the front of the building. Rawlings was walking out, alone, carrying his briefcase. He hopped in his car and pulled out of the lot.

We followed him into the city to a parking garage and then to the Bankers Trust Building on 49th and Park. Emile let me out of his car and instructed me to watch the building while he parked. Fifteen minutes later my cell rang.

"I'm on Madison, behind the building. You stay focused on Park Avenue and 49th Street and I'll watch from the Madison Avenue side on 48th."

"Okay but what if he comes out and gets in a car?"

"I've got a driver circling the block."

"Plus expenses?"

"You bet. Doesn't come out of my earnings."

"What a racket."

"Says the hedge fund manager."

Four hours later we'd followed Rawlings to two other midtown office buildings. As far as we could tell, everything seemed on the up and up.

At 5:30 he came out of a building at 53rd and Lex. I spotted him first and called Emile. "He's out and hopping into a cab."

"Okay, our driver is right behind you on 54th. Keep your eye on Rawlings' cab and follow him. The driver should be coming up to you soon."

"Okay, I've got him."

"Follow Rawlings. Don't lose him. And this is Manhattan. He won't notice that you're on his tail, so stay close. I'll get our car from the garage."

Thirty seconds later I hopped into the back of a black Town Car and said, "Follow that car." My joke was lost on the young driver, but he followed nonetheless.

Rawlings' cab stopped on 2nd Avenue and 26th Street, a middle-income residential area, not the normal stomping grounds of an ultra-wealthy private equity guy. I had my car stop on the opposite side of 2nd, the east side, and waited. Rawlings paid his cabbie and walked west on the south side of 26th Street. I followed from well behind on the north side.

Two-thirds of the way across the block he went into a small residential building, a three-storey walkup. I took out my phone and pretended to talk, occasionally glancing his way. Rawlings was standing in the public inner hallway, looking for the correct number on a panel of apartment call buttons. He appeared to push one and waited. Twenty seconds later he opened the inner door, walked inside and disappeared.

I dialed Coulon and updated him. He told me to keep talking and casually glance at the street side apartment windows, to see if I could catch a glimpse of Rawlings. I didn't.

Emile told me to walk further west, toward 3rd and wait there, but to keep my eye on the front door of the walkup.

Thirty minutes later as I stood near the northeast corner of 26th and 3rd, I felt something poke me in the back, right between my shoulder blades. A deep voice said, "Stick 'em up."

I leapt two feet forward then twisted to see who was holding the gun. It was Coulon. He was standing there with his right arm still raised and his index finger pointing out and his thumb pointing up. He was laughing so hard people on the sidewalk were turning to look at him.

"Jesus, Emile. You scared the shit out of me."

"Yeah. No kidding, you nearly jumped out of your shoes."

"Jerk."

He kept laughing.

"Shouldn't we be maintaining a low profile?

"Nah. We're fine up here. It's a good spot. We can see the front of his building and watch for anyone coming or going, but no one from inside the apartments can see us. They'd have to open a window and stick their heads out to see us from this angle."

He went on. "And while these small walkups have fire exits, they typically only lead to a courtyard in the back."

"Then I'm positive he's still in there. I haven't taken my eyes off the front of the building since I got here."

Emile smiled. "Great. I'm parked right over there. Between 3rd and Lex. Why don't you go wait in the car? I'll stand by 2nd and keep an eye on things. There's a coffee shop on the corner. Over there." He pointed to the southwest corner. "Get us some takeout and use the bathroom if you need to."

"You want me to buy you food?"

He grinned and tossed me the keys.

Two hours later my phone buzzed.

"He's heading your way on 26th, on the south side. Start the car and get ready. If he grabs a cab on 3rd, I want you to follow him. If he walks, I will. Chances are he's either going to a late dinner or to the parking garage on 51st, where he parked this morning."

"Should I pick you up?"

"No. If he gets in a cab, I'm going to hang around here and try to figure out who he saw. Let me know what he's up to."

"Okay. And I see him. He's on 3rd, walking north. He's on his phone and looking around. I think he's looking for a cab."

"Just follow him. I don't think anything else matters today. I suspect that if he's seeing someone, he just met her here. Like I said, just call me and let me know what he's doing."

"Okay."

A minute later Rawlings flagged down a Yellow Cab and hopped in. They headed north and I followed. Emile was right. The cab took him to the parking garage where he left his car. I parked illegally a half block away and waited. Five minutes later his Mercedes wagon pulled out and headed north. I followed as he turned and headed east toward the FDR.

I called Emile and he told me to stay with him as far as the FDR. If he got on heading south, I was to keep following him. If Rawlings went north, he was probably heading home and I could just let him go and pick up Emile on 26th Street.

Rawlings went north on the FDR, so I headed south.

Ten minutes later as I turned onto 26th Emile saw me and stepped into the middle of the street. He held up a hand to stop me and pointed at a woman getting into a car on the south side of the street. She was about fifty-five years old, unkempt and sort of dowdy-looking. I couldn't believe Rawlings was cheating on his gorgeous wife with her.

As Emile approached my car, I powered down the window.

Reading my mind he said, "That's not his mistress. She's leaving. Take her parking space."

I gave him the finger but laughed as I pulled into the spot she vacated. Some detective I was making.

After I parked, he joined me in the car and we watched the front of the apartment.

"You thought it was her? Really?"

"Shut up."

"You're doing fine."

"What do we do now?"

"We sit here and take pictures of anyone who comes out of 226 East 26th Street. We have to figure out who he saw here."

For the next few hours we sat in the car taking pictures of everyone who came in or out of the building. The inbound pictures were simply for reference, so we didn't confuse those people with people who were inside when Rawlings was there. Six people came out of the four-story walkup: an elderly couple, another unkempt woman (this one in her forties), an attractive blond in her early thirties with her infant son and a young man in his late twenties wearing running clothes.

The elderly couple returned after ninety minutes and the woman and child returned after just over an hour with a man who appeared to be her husband. The runner came back forty-five minutes after he left and then, thirty minutes later, went out again, this time dressed in jeans and a sweater. Neither he nor the unkempt woman had returned when we decided to head home for the night. Before we left, Emile walked into the building's public interior entryway and took a picture of the panel of apartment call buttons to get a record of the names there, for what they were worth.

On the way home we discussed the people we'd seen. The young mother seemed like the only one who could be a potential mistress. Emile was going to come back early the next morning and follow the woman, to try to figure out if she had any discernible ties to Rawlings.

I had to stay at my office in Greenwich for the next two days. On the third day I met Emile in the parking lot of Rawlings' office. As we sat waiting for him to arrive, he filled me in on what he'd discovered.

The young mother didn't have any apparent connection to Rawlings and neither did her husband. Coulon followed him the second day. He was a teacher at a public school ten blocks north of their apartment. Coulon had also seen some of the building's other tenants come and go. None were likely mistresses.

As we sat talking, a cab pulled up in front of the building. I glanced at the passenger. It wasn't Rawlings.

"Holy shit."

"What?"

As he asked, Emile followed my line of sight. Just as his eyes reached the cab, the passenger leaned down to the window to pay the driver.

Emile repeated, "What?"

The passenger stood. It was the runner from 226 East 26th Street.

We both watched him walk into Rawlings' office building. "You don't think?"

Emile shrugged. "Why else would Rawlings go to his place?"

And that was my first experience as a private investigator, or at least helping one. Over the next few weeks Coulon followed the young man, James Kopple. He established that Kopple was, in fact, gay. And he witnessed and photographed Rawlings meeting with Kopple several more times, including a night together at the Pierre Hotel on 61st near 5th.

While Emile hadn't been able to get any compromising pictures, he told me that given the nature of Rawlings' dalliance and his desire to keep his tastes private, the second Mrs.

Rawlings was confident that with the information Emile had provided, she would be able to secure favorable terms for her divorce.

Chapter 4:

After I helped wrap up the Rawlings case, I felt sure that Emile would want me to work with him again. He didn't. For weeks he ignored my requests to help him. In retrospect I realized he was playing me, reeling me in.

And it worked. He understood my itch.

Throughout my career, even when I was young and on a steep learning curve, I felt there had to be something more. Trading did provide a tremendous challenge and at times it was exhilarating to have money and my reputation on the line, to try to match my skills against other traders and markets. But after a while, it all seemed trivial. After fifteen years of working for a bank on Wall Street, I thought running my own investment fund my own way would fulfil me. But it didn't either. The walls of my office were closing in. There had to be something more interesting than trying to make money.

I occasionally talked to Jenny about it and while she was sympathetic, she never understood the depth of my frustration. She knew I regretted not having served in the military and that I sometimes wished that instead of making a career out of making money I'd done something more meaningful, like being a cop. When I discussed things like that or the idea of helping Emile in my spare time, I could see her barely-veiled disapproval. She'd tell me to run another marathon or coach another of my sons' teams. I did those things and enjoyed them, but they didn't scratch my real itch. From the glimpses I'd had, Emile's world seemed like it might. I knew it could end up being tedious too, but I had to find something.

When Emile finely relented and offered me another chance, he didn't have to ask twice.

Most people who manage money don't have the freedom to leave their office for hours or entire days; they have to fixate on their markets. That wasn't true for me. My trading strategy was based on mathematical models I'd developed. The only inputs were the daily closing prices of the bonds I traded. To keep my performance consistent with my models, I traded as close to the daily close as liquidity would allow. Every day, sometime before the close, which was at 3pm for the contracts I traded, I'd run my models and establish levels at which trades were mandated. Then I'd call-in or eventually email my trades to the firms I dealt with. That gave me the flexibility to run my company as a one-man firm. So long as I had a laptop and a phone, I could run my models from anywhere. Once I got a given day's official closing prices, generally twenty minutes after the 3pm close, I could run my models and call in the trades for the next day. In that way, at times I could spend as much as forty-six hours away from the markets without missing a trade. It took me an hour to run my models, so for example, once I knew the settlement prices on a Monday, usually by 3:20, I could run my models and send in my trades for Tuesday. Once that was done, I could be free until I had to calculate the next day's trades, as late as 2pm on Wednesday – forty-six hours later.

While I didn't have to fixate on my markets every day, because I was a one-man firm I couldn't take weeks off at a time, the way other money managers did. I had to run my models. And I did. I ran them by myself for almost twenty-five years until the day after I was shot. In all that time, I never took more than forty-six hours away from open markets and I never missed a single trade. Cal Ripkin only lasted sixteen years and he had winters off. But for me, occasionally having those forty-six hours was important. It gave me a break from the numbers, from the pressure and gave me the flexibility to sit in cars or follow people of interest with my friend Emile.

Once Emile let me back in, I stayed. For the first few

years, I worked with him for a day or two a month, but eventually that evolved into a day or two a week. Occasionally I even traveled with him. I became a contract employee, and he paid me $70 an hour. He never gave a straight answer about what he charged his clients for my services, but knowing him, I was getting ripped off. I didn't need the money, but once I became competent, I think he felt better about bossing me around if he was paying me. And from my perspective, the years I spent working with him were invaluable. The experience literally saved my life. But I'm getting ahead of myself.

From the very beginning I loved detective work. It was fun. Emile and I did everything from investigating adultery to background checks to serving summonses. The work could be scary or tedious but mostly it was fascinating.

Emile was on retainer with a number of law firms in Connecticut and New York and some of the work we did for them was serving summonses. In some states, to serve a summons the server had to get the person being served to acknowledge his or her name and birth date. That information could be very difficult to extract from a person who didn't want to be served. Fortunately, that was not the case in Connecticut or New York. Still, serving someone who was evasive could be tricky.

Many of the summonses Coulon served were for corporate clients involved in lawsuits. In such situations, the people being summoned frequently worked for other corporations and were often working with those corporations' lawyers. Less scrupulous lawyers sometimes advised potential witnesses on how to avoid being served.

On one occasion, a former corporate treasurer we were trying to serve was being especially evasive. The man, Rick Dempsey, was an innocent witness to his bosses' theft, but didn't want to testify because he felt his career would be over if he was labeled a whistleblower. Our lawyer's client, the board and ultimately the shareholders of the corporation, needed his testimony. In the weeks leading up to the case's grand jury date, he successfully avoided us in New York, then disappeared. With only a week to go, we discovered he was at his in-laws' cottage on the northern coast of Maine. The cottage, in the small town of Sorrento, was at the end of a very long driveway and we weren't comfortable that we'd be able to surprise and serve him at the house.

After two days of waiting on a rural road near his driveway, he hadn't left the property once, at least not by car. We thought we might have better luck trying to watch him from the water, so we rented a 24-foot center console fishing boat and fished in Sullivan's Bay, across from Dempsey's shoreline property. At its widest, the bay was almost two miles across, so we were easily able to hide in plain sight.

Emile loved to fish and was in heaven. As we bobbed along, he commented knowingly on every boat that passed, and described his dream fishing boat, a 38-foot Boston Whaler Outrage. When I asked him why he didn't just buy one, he scoffed and said the one he wanted, rigged right, would cost more than his house.

In fairly short order, our fishing and detecting efforts were rewarded. An hour or so after we landed our third black sea bass, the treasurer, his wife and in-laws got into their boat and headed out the bay, toward Bar Harbor. We easily followed from a considerable distance. Our plan was to trail Dempsey's boat to wherever it docked and serve him there.

The treasurer's father-in-law was at the helm. He guided his boat past Bar Harbor and headed toward the outer islands and the Atlantic, further south and east. They were in a thirty-six-foot Hinckley Picnic Boat, built just miles away and designed to easily cut the rolling swells pounding the exposed coast. Our twenty-four-footer was fine, but rather than knifing though the four- to six-foot rollers, we rode over them and slammed down off their backs. After fifty brain-jarring minutes, the Hinckley turned in toward the small islands off the coast. The calmer waters behind the islands were a welcome relief.

We tailed them to Little Cranberry Island. They tied up at the public dock. We followed about ten minutes behind. By the time we had secured our boat, we could see the treasurer and his family walking inland, along the only street leading from the harbor.

Little Cranberry Island isn't big – at best it's a mile long and a half-mile wide. Rather than following them onto the island, where they would almost surely notice us, we decided to wait near the dock. We'd serve him when he came back to his boat.

We waited in the Islesford Dock Restaurant, an open-air place built right over the dock. We ordered sandwiches and sat at the bar, nursing beers and watching.

A little over an hour later Dempsey and his family were heading back our way. We paid our bill and followed them toward the boats. They made their way down the dock, which was essentially one structure, three hundred feet long with several smaller docks branching off to the inland side. Their Hinckley was tied to the end of the main dock.

When they were fifty feet from their boat and past the second to last small branching dock, Emile walked past them. I lagged behind. Emile turned and faced them. Dempsey, who had been talking with his mother-in-law, looked up at Emile and then at the light-brown, legal-sized envelope he was holding. Then he turned and saw me behind him.

He realized we had him. He could either run around me or jump in the water. But this was northern Maine in May; the water temperature was probably in the forties. At best, even in late August when the water is at its warmest, people dove in for seconds. In May, even seconds were dangerous.

Dempsey looked at me again, evaluating his options. Then, to everyone's surprise, he dove in. I don't know what his plan was. Perhaps he thought he could swim out into the bay and have his father-in-law pick him up and then they'd go back to the safety of their cottage until after the Grand Jury convened.

But no one can stay in such frigid water for that long. He swam for two or three strokes before realizing it was pointless. He turned and swam back.

This was an innocent man guilty of only trying not to ruin his career by ratting out criminals.

Ten seconds after he jumped in, he was back at the dock. I went to him and extended my hand. He looked up at me, his eyes resigned, and took it. As I pulled him up onto the dock Emile stepped forward, handed him the envelope and told him he'd been served.

I think that was the only time I ever heard regret in Emile's voice.

Chapter 5:

For the next twelve years I helped Emile as often as I could. I liked him. He was different. His work was different.

My other friends weren't. They were the same. We were the same. We'd gone to school together, worked together, shared weddings and births and raised our kids together. We were well-educated, well-traveled, well-employed and mostly white. We cared about our wives, our children, their educations, our communities and our country. We were bland and predictable.

My life was tedious. When I discussed it with Jenny, she said my complaining was tedious. And she had a point. I could have tried to fulfill myself by working harder at my real job, marketing more aggressively, tweaking my models or even exploring other possibilities. But that was just more of the same. Once I'd built my company to a level that provided my family with financial freedom, the pursuit of money lost its allure. I wanted more. And when I say more, I mean something else.

Emile offered that "more". As it turned out, more than I ever imagined. He wanted to make money as much as the next guy, but that wasn't what drove him. To him, everything was personal.

Many of the people Emile watched led innocent lives, but they had at least one secret to hide. Emile loved that. He viewed them as adversaries and pitted himself against them. They were trying to get away with something and he was trying to figure out what it was. It was a mental battle between him and them. The smartest person won.

The stakes weren't high for Emile. If he discovered his adversary's secret he got paid, if he didn't, he still got paid. But for the people he investigated, the stakes were massive. Emile could ruin their reputations, their careers, their marriages, sometimes even take away their freedom.

He loved that and, as much as I hate to admit it, I did too. The analytics behind detective work were like trading on steroids. I figured policemen felt the same thrill, but they were at least acting in the public interest. There was nothing altruistic behind my fascination. These people had dark secrets they were trying to hide. They plotted to prevent anyone from finding them out. I loved looking into their lives and figuring them out, uncovering the thing they'd tried so carefully to conceal. The smartest person won. Emile was right. It was personal.

I tried to explain it all to Jenny but couldn't get her to understand. That frustrated both of us because even though we looked at things from different perspectives, we respected each other's opinions and usually, eventually reached the same conclusions. In most areas of my life, she was my best advisor and sounding board. While her eyes glazed over when I described the math behind my models, when I needed help in other areas, I talked to her. She was the other half of my team. But she couldn't support or begin to condone my frustration or my career wanderlust. Her view was that everyone had to do shit they didn't like and that few people could do everything they wanted. I was a husband and a father with responsibilities. I should just man up and deal with it.

I knew she was right. Nonetheless I continued to work with Emile.

Chapter 6:

In the beginning, Emile shielded me from his more danger-ous work. The worst secrets I sussed out dealt with infidelity or, occasionally, white collar crime.

Our clients were often companies vetting prospective em-ployees. They hired us to look into candidates' financial, em-ployment, educational and legal histories, to confirm that the pictures the prospects painted were honest. Often times, for things like college transcripts, the candidate had to authorize access, so it was rare to find material discrepancies. And for the level of jobs we were dealing with, the candidates likely knew that the information they provided would be verified so they tended to be fairly honest. But there were exceptions.

Given that New York and Greenwich were centers for asset management firms and hedge funds, a lot of the background checks we did were in that area. In investment management, people often took disproportionate credit for exaggerated per-formance records generated by team efforts. We all have dif-ferent perspectives on how much we contribute to things, so there was room for some ambiguity. Our job was to question former colleagues and bosses, to get some idea of a candidate's true contribution to performance. Even with traders whose performance numbers weren't publicly available, we could get some sense of the returns the person generated through tax re-cords. For example, if he or she traded a notional $100 million and was paid 15% of earnings after salary and expenses, it was fairly simple to calculate each candidate's approximate trading revenues.

With less externally quantifiable jobs, like commercial or investment banking, it was harder to measure a person's actu-al contribution, so the bullshit factor could be considerable. And that wasn't necessarily a bad thing. While one wanted to hire a portfolio manager or trader or CFO who was generally honest and forthcoming, the same wasn't necessarily true for a salesman.

At any rate, our job was to sift through as much information as we could find and look for inconsistencies. The people who hired us decided what to do with that information.

While I found the background work interesting, it was generally pretty dry. The real fun of it was in uncovering liars. The biggest liar I discovered was a mortgage-backed securities trader named Amy Shelton. She was up for a portfolio management job in the investment division of one of the country's biggest banks. Shelton maintained that she'd left her last job at a huge fund called Milmar Partners because, in spite of the fact that she had been the primary contributor to the firm's stellar performance and meteoric growth, she'd *only* been paid $8 million. She claimed she was owed three times that. She provided tax returns confirming the $8 million, but cautioned us that because of her acrimonious departure, no one at her old firm would confirm her true contribution.

Wall Street is a small place where people know that what goes around comes around. Typically, when we called a former employer for a reference or background, even if they had a horrible experience with our subject, they'd downplay any criticism. They might offer hints, saying things like "We had different investment philosophies" or "She wanted to go in different directions than we did." But Amy's former employers were fairly forthcoming. In addition to exaggerating her contribution to performance, she omitted some seriously inappropriate behavior, even by the standards of the '80s and '90s.

Amy, who was thirty-seven and built like an offensive lineman, had undisclosed appetites. And many at that. Several of her former colleagues told us a story that had become a Wall Street legend. Apparently one night she had dinner with two white-shoed, Ivy-League-educated Morgan Stanley bond salesmen at a trendy Tribeca restaurant. The men, dressed in conservative business suits, were surprised and embarrassed when Amy walked in. She was wearing a mid-thigh, skin-tight, bridal-white, silky-looking cocktail dress that would have made Stormy Daniels blush. The entire restaurant stopped and watched as she was escorted to the poor guys' table. While they were mortified by the attention, she seemed to enjoy it. Still, she was a mortgage trader for one of the biggest funds on the street and they wanted her business, so they politely got through the dinner. And while Amy enjoyed the dinner, eating like a lineman, she had additional plans for her two hosts. Sometime around the dessert course, she pointedly asked them to join her for a threesome at a nearby hotel. While the men were able to politely dissuade her, the story of her efforts quickly made its way around Wall Street.

Her needs unsated, Amy redirected her peculiar charm to a younger male assistant at her own firm. He was receptive. For a year or two during many a quiet trading day, the two would not-so-subtly steal away and spend an hour or two at a nearby hotel and return minutes apart, rosy-cheeked and smiling, having fooled no one.

But Amy's sexual appetites were not what brought her down. Her employers were willing to overlook those short-comings so long as her investment performance was acceptable. And for a while it clearly was.

But I knew she was hiding something. So were the people at Milmar. While her former colleagues were willing to discuss her sexual activities, they weren't as forthcoming about her trading or her integrity. I could tell they were holding back, so I looked beyond the firm to ex-employees. I found a retired Milmar executive who was willing to talk.

The man, a blunt speaking sixty-seven-year-old named

Fred Selinsky had been Milmar's head of compliance. He explained that in the days prior to her dismissal, Amy made unauthorized trades in highly volatile, principal-only (PO) strips on mortgage-backed securities. She had pitched the idea to her colleagues, but they rejected it. Angered by what she perceived as their stupidity, she decided to ignore the firm's trading rules and buy the POs for a few small accounts. Three days after she implemented the trade, interest rates rose sharply and her unauthorized positions went horribly against her. Rather than cutting her losses and owning up, she tried to hide the trades. She reallocated the losing positions from the three small accounts to one huge account where she felt they might go unnoticed. Her reallocation days after the trade date set off more alarms than the losses alone would have. And it broke laws. The compliance department immediately alerted senior management and they called Amy in. She claimed that she thought her colleagues had agreed she could implement the PO trades on a small scale and that she had simply made an honest mistake with the reallocation.

Management told her to take a couple of days off and had other traders close out the PO trades. A few days later they told her to come back to work, but to report to the executive offices on the 27th floor. Amy was led to a conference room and met by her immediate boss, the firm's chief counsel and Selinsky. Amy's boss led with, "We've decided not to press charges."

She was fired for breaking ERISA laws and for lying about her trades. Milmar made the small accounts whole and took the losses on the POs themselves. They withheld the deferred portion of her prior years bonuses to help cover those losses.

Chapter 7:

Even Emile was impressed with the work I'd done to uncover all of Amy's shit. After that he made me an unofficial part of his team.

The other official member of his team was his assistant, Beverly Sutton. Like her boss, Bev was a piece of work and a skilled ball-buster. She was 5'11", three inches taller than Emile, and had a personality that could stand up to his. She had a thick Boston accent and a thicker shtick. That shtick could be hilarious or frightening. When Bev was in a good mood, which I'd seen two or three times over the years, she could almost be friendly. But most of the time she attacked anyone in her path with a cutting wit that mirrored her dark mood. She was funny as hell – so long as she wasn't focused on you.

I never really understood Emile and Bev's relationship. Emile had been married twice during the time I knew him. The first marriage was in its final stages when Jenny and I met him back in '94 and the second, which started in '01, was an eighteen-month nightmare with a former client.

Between marriages and girlfriends, Emile and Beverly periodically took comfort together. That was a fact I hadn't detected and which I discovered in an indelible incident that happened in July of 1999, five years into my friendship with Emile.

My wife Jenny and I have four grown sons. For ten years when they were young, we rented a house on Squam Lake in New Hampshire for the month of July. I tried to spend the entire month there, but inevitably would have to go home or to New York once or twice to deal with work issues. It was on such a trip that I first discovered Emile and Bev's other relationship.

I drove from New Hampshire to Connecticut on a Tuesday evening to prepare for a new client pitch on Thursday. Originally, I'd planned to go straight to our home in New Canaan and put my pitch together the following morning. But as I approached my exit at 9pm, I was so wired on Diet Coke and junk food that I decided to go to the office for a couple of hours.

I got to Greenwich at 9:20 and predictably, my building looked pretty empty. As I approached my office, I saw the lights were still on in Emile's office. Unlike my windowless, a ten-by-twelve-foot glass-fronted box, his business occupied three rooms: a reception area where Beverly had her desk, Emile's office and a small conference room.

I opened the door and walked into his reception area. It was empty. I figured Bev was long gone and that Emile was probably working late in his office. By that time we were close friends and I didn't see a need to knock on his office door, especially at that hour. I should have.

I opened the door and was about to make some snide comment, but instead stopped dead in my tracks. Emile and Bev were in front of his desk. Well, Emile was in front of his desk. Bev was bent over it.

His desk was on the right side of his office so when they heard the door open, they each looked over their left shoulders. Emile froze, we all did. For what couldn't have been more than an instant, we didn't move. I should have been the first to react, to retreat, but I was so shocked that these two apparent adversaries weren't actually adversaries that I couldn't. After perhaps a few seconds, their shock turned to anger and they both swayed their heads toward the door, gesturing for me to get the hell out. Finally, I unfroze and backed out muttering "I'm sorry." I pulled the door closed behind me and headed straight to my office. I sat at my desk staring blankly forward, processing what I'd seen.

After a minute or two I looked out through the glass that was the front wall of my office at the door to Emile's offices. I realized that the only way Bev could leave was through that door. I didn't want to embarrass her further or, more honestly, I didn't want to face her fury, so I grabbed my briefcase and ran for the safety of my car and home.

The next morning, I was at work by 6:30. At 8:50 I saw Bev walking down the hall. Without looking in my direction she started to go into her office, but halfway in, seemed to change her mind. She turned and walked into my office.

The ball-busting blonde looked me straight in the eyes and said, "Good morning."

I looked up from the work I was pretending to do. "Morning."

She held her gaze considering her response, then shook her head, laughed and simply said, "Fuck."

Chapter 8:

Years later, in October of 2007, Emile called and asked me to meet him at his office. By then my office was in a different part of Greenwich, in Riverside on the Mianus River. Emile was still in the same spot by the train station. I told him I'd be there at four after I'd settled the trades I was doing that afternoon.

At ten to four I walked into Emile's reception area. Bev was sitting at her desk.

"Afternoon."

She looked up at me with an uncharacteristically concerned expression on her face but nonetheless responded, "Hey, Dickhead. He's in there."

I walked past her and, largely for her sake, tapped on his office door then slowly opened it. Normally at a minimum she would have flipped me the bird. She didn't. She looked worried. Something was up.

I looked inside.

In spite of the nature of our work, it rarely involved violence. And when it might, Emile tried not to involve me.

Violence is an interesting thing. Typically, it's either part of your life or not. Fortunately for most of us, it's not. We see it on television and read about it in the news and in books, but it doesn't touch us. And for those of us who live largely non-violent lives, it's not something we think much about. But when I started to work with Emile, I did consider it. Even with him sheltering me, things sometimes got a little tense, people sometimes got angry. But usually, the anger was manifested verbally or at the very most with a push or shove.

When push did come to shove, my comfort level waned. I was a fit man, but for me fitness meant being able to run far and fast. When I went to a gym, I went straight to a treadmill. I cranked up the speed and ran. Others went to the weight room and lifted. I got faster and they got stronger. Was I subconsciously training to run away while they were training to fight?

The more I thought about it, the more uncomfortable I became. I liked to believe I could protect my wife and children. I actually had some confidence that I could. At the very least I felt I'd use myself as a shield against would-be attackers, to give the people I cared most about a chance to get away.

But those are the thoughts of a rational man, a peaceful man. Thugs didn't think that way. They played offense. I contemplated defense.

To the extent I could, I put those negative thoughts aside and hoped that I could work as a private detective without dealing with violence. For thirteen years, I had.

Then I walked into Emile's office.

He was sitting behind his desk enveloped in a stark-white plaster cast that virtually covered his torso, from his left shoulder over the upper portion of his chest and back, and then across and over to his right arm and all the way to his right wrist. A metal brace was built into the plaster to hold his arm up. He had stitches over his left eye and dark bruising all over his face. If he wasn't sitting at his desk, I'm not sure I would have recognized him.

"What happened?"

"I got into something I shouldn't have."

"What was it? What do you mean?"

"It doesn't matter. You know how it is. Sometimes we run into the wrong people."

"I don't know how it is. What are you talking about?"

Even after all these years, I had a feeling there were significant parts of Emile's work that I knew nothing about.

"Just another irate husband I caught cheating, nothing to worry about. That's not why I asked you in."

"Nothing to worry about? Are you kidding me? Look at you."

"It's just a flesh wound." He started to laugh and then grimaced and reached for his ribs with his good hand. "Oh God, it hurts to laugh. I have a few cracked ribs as well."

"Who did this to you?"

"It doesn't matter, Phil. I'm sorry to say it's a part of the business. Every once in a while, I get incriminating information on the wrong guy."

"What guy?" Thoughts were racing through my mind. The first was that whoever did it should be behind bars. "Where did it happen? Did you call the police?"

"No. Fuck no. We don't call the police."

"Why not? It's not like we're doing anything illegal."

He raised his voice, something he rarely did. "We can't call the police."

I had the feeling that Emile was hiding something truly meaningful from me. He seemed to read my thoughts.

"Look. If we call the police, it'll make the papers and we can't have that."

"Why? Who cares? You've done nothing wrong." My last sentence came out as more of a question than a statement of fact.

Emile paused for a little too long, then said. "Of course not. I just can't afford that sort of publicity. As you well know, most of my business is with law firms and corporations and the rest comes from wealthy, law-abiding husbands and wives. I don't want any of them to see this side of things. They'll think of us as seedy and go to bigger, more established firms. It's hard enough for people to hire a private detective, we can't let them think we're any dirtier than they already do."

"So you lose a few squeamish clients. Who cares?"

"It wouldn't just be a few. Do you think the law firms or

headhunters or asset management firms would hire me if they thought I was going to interview their clients or prospective employees looking like this?"

"I see your point. But if word gets out that husbands can beat you up, break your arm and crack your ribs without repercussion, what's going to happen to you? What's the next guy going to do? And don't think for a second that once the dust settles and the guy who did this realizes you're not calling the cops on him that he won't brag about beating you up."

Emile considered his reply for a minute. "I'm not worried about that. I'll deal with him."

"You'll deal with him?" I was incredulous. "How?"

"Don't worry about it."

"Don't worry about it? Are you fucking kidding? I work with you. My reputation is on the line too. How are you going to deal with it? What are you going to do, hire some thug to beat him up for you?"

Again, he paused before answering.

"Don't be ridiculous. Like I said, I can't afford to have any of this in the paper. If I hired some guy to beat up a client's husband and that got out, it'd be worse than everyone knowing I got beat up."

"Then what are you going to do?"

"I'm going to send the guy who assaulted me a letter, one my lawyer and I drafted. In it, I explain that at this point I've decided not to go to the police because the publicity would be bad for everyone. But the letter makes it clear that while some negative publicity would be bad for me, he'd be facing jail time or at least a police enquiry. He broke the law. I did not."

Emile let that sink in. "The guy's an exec with a big company. He can't afford for that to happen. I'll tell him that so long as he pays my medical bills, I'll keep it to myself."

"Do you think he will?"

"I'm not sure, but I think so. This happened three days ago. He must be at home sweating, waiting for the police to knock on his door. We, my lawyer and I, decided to wait one more day before we have the letter delivered."

"How about this guy's wife? Does he have kids? If he beat you up over this, aren't you worried about her?"

The question caught him by surprise, which surprised me.

"Haven't you warned her?"

"No. I can't look after every woman in Fairfield County. It's not my problem."

"Not your problem?"

He saw my reaction and backtracked. "The guy's worried about the police arresting him for assaulting me. There's no way he's going to compound his problems by beating his wife. We don't have to worry about that."

"I don't know how you can be so sure. You should call her."

"I'm sure she already knows. It was after she showed him the pictures I sent her that he came after me. If he was going to hurt her, he'd have done it by now. Besides, she didn't warn me he was coming."

"That's mature. Christ, Emile."

"Alright. I'll have Bev call her."

We sat for a moment before he realized I was waiting for him to get Bev to do it. He called her in and told her to call the woman – whose name Bev apparently was privy to – and to tell her that her husband had come to see him and that he had been agitated. Bev and I both recoiled at his understatement, but he reiterated his words and assured us that they would be sufficient to get his point across without undermining his efforts to keep the incident from escalating. He didn't want to do anything that would further incite the husband.

After Bev left, he said, "Now you can see why I demand a $2500 deposit up front. Can you imagine how hard it would be to collect after the spouse finds out? Especially a spouse like this asshole."

"Yeah. You're right. Even if the spouse didn't get violent, I'm sure he or she wouldn't be in a hurry to pay you."

"Exactly." Emile just sat for a moment, giving me a chance to settle down. "The reason I wanted to see you is that I'm going to need your help with some clients for a week or two until I'm more presentable. I have some meetings set up with law firms, a bank and a couple of head-hunting companies. They're follow-up meetings, all stuff you can easily handle. As I said, I don't want them to see me looking like this. And I don't want to postpone meetings with them because I'm afraid I'll lose the business. It's more work than I've ever asked you to do and I wouldn't ask if I didn't really need you. Do you think you can do it?"

"Will they care that you're not doing the follow up?"

"Nah. Actually, let's tell them that I was in a minor car accident. Nothing too serious but that I'm a little beat up."

"I'm not going to lie."

"Fucking boy scout. Fine, just tell them I'm under the weather. Are you comfortable with that?"

His tone was sarcastic.

"Who's asking who for a favor here?"

"Okay, okay. Sorry."

He tried to get things back on his track. "You've met some of them and even with those you haven't, you'll be fine. Will you do it? Can you step in?"

"Sure. I'll take care of it."

Chapter 9:

Emile's recovery took longer than he expected. He ended up needing surgery on his left arm which had been broken in several places. So I filled in for the meetings we'd discussed and took the lead role in the subsequent investigations.

During his convalescence I spent a lot of time in his office in Greenwich, often working out of his conference room. I got a sense of the daily flow of his business and saw many of the people who stopped by to meet with him or Bev. It had been years since my office was across the hall, so there were a lot of new faces. I asked Bev about some of them, but she told me it was none of my business. She said that if Emile had wanted me to know about every aspect of his business, he'd have told me and that since he hadn't, she had no business telling me. I couldn't argue with her logic.

A month into Emile's convalescence, an attorney from one of his client law firms, Fort & Clarence, asked if I could stop by her office at 8pm. The lawyer, Patty Mahoney, had been traveling and wanted to brief me on some work she needed done. Mahoney was extremely busy and after we concluded our work, she asked me to find my own way out.

Even at that late hour there were a few other lawyers and some paralegals and assistants in their offices or at their desks. The cleaning crew was also there, dusting desks, vacuuming carpets and emptying trash cans. I was surprised to recognize one member of the cleaning crew, the man who seemed to be in charge. I'd seen him at Emile's office. He wasn't a big man, but he carried himself with a real air of authority. He was in his sixties, but in great shape and full of energy. He was talking in a foreign language to one of the women on his staff, giving her instructions. As I walked past, they both looked up. He and I made eye contact. At first his face showed a hint of concern, but he gathered himself and smiled. I think he recognized me, but I wasn't sure he realized I was from Emile's office. I smiled and nodded but kept walking.

That night I couldn't stop thinking about the coincidence of him being at the law firm and at Emile's office. The few times I had seen him, he and Bev had gone into Emile's office to discuss business. While Bev didn't treat anyone especially nicely, she treated clients with some deference. She hadn't treated the cleaning man that way. My sense was that he worked for her, or rather, for Emile. And not as a cleaner.

Something seemed off.

The next morning I stopped by Emile's office. I got there at ten and Bev was sitting at her desk. She was used to me coming by at all hours of the day, whenever I had free time, so she wasn't surprised.

"Morning, Bev."

"Hey, Phil."

I stood by her desk. "Last night I met with Patty Mahoney, over at Fort & Clarence."

"How'd that go? Anything we need to brief Emile about?"

"No. Just another background check."

"Great." She looked down at her work, trying to dismiss me.

"Funny thing happened there. I saw a guy I've seen here a few times over the last month."

I watched her face closely to see if she'd react at all. She didn't.

"Who?"

"I don't know his name. Nice-looking older guy, maybe Greek? About sixty but fit?"

"I don't know, Phil, we have a lot of clients."

Her tone showed her normal impatience, no sign of covering anything up.

"He worked on the cleaning crew there. I think he ran it."

Bev thought for a second and then said, "Oh sure. I know who you mean."

"Who is he?"

"One of Emile's clients. Not one of the ones you work with."

Bev lied. I normally considered her a straight shooter, but she flat out lied. She could have just said that it was none of my business and I would have walked away. But she didn't. She lied. She was hiding something.

I left the office, seething.

For the next few weeks I continued to manage Emile's client relationships, because I told him I would. But after his beating, his casual disregard for his attacker's wife and the incident with Bev, I considered quitting. Things were going too far. While I always had a sense that Emile was willing to cut corners, I never thought he was dishonest. I wouldn't have worked with him if I did. But now I wasn't so sure.

Chapter 10:

When Emile finally did come back, I asked him about the guy from the cleaning service. He told me that the man was a client who had asked him to look into the activities of his business partner who was also his brother. He said the guy was terrified that his brother would find out about the investigation and had asked to deal only with Emile.

That seemed plausible, so in spite of my gut reservations, I stayed on. In my heart I knew I shouldn't have, that Emile was up to more than he was letting on, but the work I did for him was the most interesting part of my life. I didn't want to give it up. In some sense, I couldn't.

By that time, in early 2008, my fund business was well established and my client base was stable. I managed a total of about $55 million for a handful of clients. For years I had tried to expand, but that was difficult for a one-person firm. Even if they were interested in my performance track record, most larger prospects felt I was too small to risk investing with. They frequently said, call us back when you get $250 million under management or a billion. Even funds with bigger staffs faced the same issue. I became content with the size of my business and while I spent lots of time making sure my existing clients were getting the exact amount of attention they wanted, I didn't spend much time trying to expand – I had sort of hit the wall there. And with $55 million under management, I was making a good living.

Later that year, before the financial crisis hit, I was spending about a third of my time working for Emile, managing the day-to-day relationships with many of his corporate and institutional clients. Emile told them he was in charge and that he oversaw everything I did, but the reality was more complicated. He was spending less and less time in the Greenwich office. He said he'd picked up a big account in Chicago and opened an office there. Details were typically thin.

As I became the corporate face of his Greenwich business and my name became increasingly tied to his, my discomfort with what he wasn't telling me increased. As a one-man firm, if my name was associated with even a hint of a scandal, my fund business and revenue would disappear. I was making over seven figures every year from the hedge fund business and only tens of thousands from my work with Emile. No matter how much I liked detective work, I was a husband and a father of four. A million dollars a year was hard to overlook.

When I tried to discuss my concerns with Emile, he brushed me off. When I discussed them with Jenny, she implored me to walk away. In spite of all of the warning signals, I held on.

In the meantime, things in the financial world got hairy. In 2008 when the US economy imploded, most hedge funds got beat up. I had a good year. But 2009 was a different story. As the US economy continued to deteriorate, the Fed initiated a second round of quantitative easing. They hoped to keep the economy afloat by keeping interest rates artificially low. The combination was brutal for me. Markets were volatile, but in a narrow range. My strategy was getting eaten alive. I had to stay in my office, readily available, should any of my long-standing clients have questions. I told Emile, who was spending most of his time in Chicago, that I had to focus on my fund business. He understood and took over the accounts I was running for him.

The universe solved my problem for me. But only in the short run.

Chapter 11:

I couldn't leave well-enough alone. When financial markets stabilized and my need to be laser focused on my fund business receded, I became increasingly unsettled. It wasn't lost on me that I found trading more interesting when I was struggling than when I was succeeding, but I didn't know what to make of that.

I did know that once again, I needed more. I also knew I should stay away from Emile. But I didn't. After a few months of telling Jenny that I wouldn't go back, I did.

One of the relationships I handled was with the Stamford office of a major New York law firm, Dewey, Grant & Howe. Emile had a very good relationship with one of the firm's senior partners, an engaging man named Kim Campbell. Campbell worked at the firm's headquarters in New York, but lived in Connecticut and occasionally used his firm's Stamford office.

One of Campbells's clients, a New York-based asset management firm called Bay Street Partners, was considering buying Dunvegan Investments, a smaller firm. While accounting and investment banking firms would check Dunvegan's financials, our role was to get more granular by talking with their clients, counterparties and former employees to look for any irregularities. Bay Street was interested in Dunvegan because of its high-yield fixed income team, led by a man named Aaron Goodchild. Our role was to learn as much about Goodchild and his team as we could.

With my background in fixed income, it was a natural job for me and during the few meetings he attended, I had a sense that Kim Campbell was pleased with my work. For my part it was easy to see why Kim was so successful. He was extremely hard-working and a natural leader but had an easygoing manner and an outgoing personality. And he had the same sort of magnetism and zest for life as Emile.

One day in June of 2010, five weeks into the Dunvegan project, Campbell's assistant summoned me to his office. She told me to bring all of my work and files relating to the Bay Street/Dunvegan deal with me.

Ninety minutes later I entered the green-marbled reception area of Dewey, Grant & Howe. One of the normally engaging receptionists ignored my friendly greeting and quietly led me to a conference room. Contrary to what I had come to view as the firm's normal protocol, she didn't offer me any sort of refreshments or let me know who I would be meeting with or when they would be joining me. She simply closed the door and left. Forty minutes later one of Dewey's attorneys who was working on the case, Dick Bourgeois, came in. Rather than shaking hands or offering any sort of cordial greeting, Bourgeois simply sat down across the table from me and curtly instructed that I summarize my findings with regard to the Bay Street/Dunvegan deal. I presented our findings, which were favorable, without a single interruption. Once I finished my presentation, Bourgeois instructed me to stop all work on behalf of Dewey with regard to the Bay Street deal and two other smaller investigations.

He handed me a formal termination letter which he asked me to read and sign.

I was flabbergasted.

"Why are you terminating us?"

"We no longer need your services. Please sign the agreement."

"You know I can't sign this. What's going on?"

"If you can't sign it, take it to your boss." Bourgeois, normally a reserved man, said 'boss' with clear disdain.

"What's going on, Dick? What happened?"

He didn't soften at all. He gathered the papers I had given him and went to the door of the conference room. He opened it and a security guard stepped into the doorway.

"Escort Mr. Osgood from the building."

He left without looking back.

I couldn't believe what was happening. Emile was in Chicago, so I called him from my car. When I told him we'd been terminated by Dewey, he didn't seem all that surprised or upset. I asked him what had happened, but he said he didn't know. Even on the phone I could tell he was lying. He said he'd call Campbell, but I doubted he would.

Enough was finally enough. Whatever Emile was doing, I could no longer be a part of it. I had to sever all my ties with him.

The next morning, I called Emile and told him that I had decided to stop working with him because I wasn't comfortable with what was going on. He didn't ask for an explanation. After fifteen years he just accepted it with the same cold detachment he had exhibited in reaction to the Dewey news.

When he and Bev flew back east, I got them up to speed on the accounts I was managing. We parted somewhat amicably, promising to stay in touch.

Chapter 12:

Two years later, in 2012, a friend named Paul Bamatter started a fund with five other traders. They leased the top floor of a small standalone building in downtown Greenwich. Paul asked if I wanted to rent an extra office they had. I liked Paul and his partners, and the space was great, so I moved my office there. By that time everything was internet based so I didn't have to climb up onto the roof to install any satellite dishes.

One afternoon six months after I moved in, I was sitting at my desk, reading. My office was near the end of a hallway, and I didn't get a lot of unexpected traffic, so I was startled as two thuggish-looking guys filled my doorway.

The smaller of the two, a man in his late forties, six feet tall and maybe two hundred and thirty solid-looking pounds, said "You Osgood?"

"Yes. How can I help you?"

"Where's Coulon?"

My office was an oddly shaped room, seven by twelve feet. My built-in desk ran along the entire outer wall, so there wasn't much floor space inside. The room could only comfortably accommodate one person: me. If I met clients or wanted to sit and talk with anyone else, I generally did it in the conference room. At any rate there wasn't room for three people.

The apparent leader of the two, the guy in his forties, took advantage of that. He stepped up close to me, effectively forcing me and my wheeled office chair back against the desk as I faced outwards toward him. I tried to stand but he got closer, making it impossible.

"I asked you a question."

I tried to stand again, irritated. "Who are you?"

He pushed me back into my chair.

"Where is fucking Coulon?"

I didn't want to throw Emile under the bus, but I figured if they found my office, they must know where his was.

"I assume he's at his office."

"He hasn't been there in weeks. Where the fuck is he?"

The first guy was all the way in my office, towering over me, but the second guy, a huge guy in his late thirties, was still in the doorway. Two of the men sitting on the six-man trading desk just down the hallway heard the raised voices and came to see what was going on.

Any bravado they had diminished when they saw the 6'5", 260-pound thug in my doorway glance over his massive shoulder as he heard them approach.

The first of the traders, my friend Paul, stopped a few feet from the doorway and asked, "Is everything alright, Phil?"

I looked up at the man in front of me and tried to stand up, again. He pushed his palm sharply forward into my forehead, shoving me back into my seat.

"He's fine. Fuck off."

He could have just as easily slammed his palm into my nose and broken it, but he didn't. He just wanted my attention.

From the hallway Paul yelled, "Should I call the police?"

The older thug looked down at me.

I looked him in the eyes and with surprising calm responded, "Not yet."

By now two more of Paul's colleagues had joined him in the hallway, but they were all five feet back from the younger thug, who'd turned to face them. His calmness staring down four men was menacing.

"Where's Coulon?"

"I don't know. I haven't seen him in a long time."

"How can that be? You work with him."

"I don't. I used to help him sometimes, but I haven't for a couple of years."

"Where's Bev?"

Now I was concerned. While I knew Emile spent most of his time in Chicago, I thought Bev was still working out of Greenwich.

"I don't know. As I said, I haven't worked with them since 2010."

"Neither has set foot in their offices here or in Chicago in over three weeks. Where are they?"

"I told you, I don't have any idea."

He stood looking down at me. My sense was that he was just on a fact-finding mission and didn't want it to escalate into a scene involving the police. More importantly, I think he believed me.

"If you see him or talk to him, tell him Geordie Hendrie is looking for him."

I'd never met Hendrie, but I knew who he was. Everyone in the New York area did. He ran organized crime in Westchester and Duchess counties in New York and throughout western Connecticut. And his name had come up in some work I'd done for Emile six or seven years earlier.

"Understood?"

"Yes."

With that he and his associate stepped from my office and walked toward Paul and his three colleagues, who were still standing in the hall near the exit door. The four men backed off, down the hall into the open trading area and were visibly relieved when, rather than continuing toward them, the two thugs turned and went out the door. As soon as they were out and could be heard clomping down the stairs to the street, Paul and his team hurried back to my office. I was standing in the doorway, but surprisingly, not shaken.

"Who the hell was that?" He was seriously pissed off.

"Honestly, Paul, I have no idea."

"Are you going to call the police?"

I thought about it for a moment. "No. But I better call the guy they're looking for."

Emile's cell rang three times then went to voice mail. I left a message then tried his Greenwich and Chicago offices and finally Bev's cell. No one answered.

I had some work to do and tried to focus on it, but I couldn't. I tried all four numbers a couple of more times and then decided to drive over to their offices. But first I googled Geordie Hendrie. There were a few listings. I opened the links related to the Hendrie I knew. They didn't tell me much beyond a residential address in Greenwich and the names of two companies he owned.

I drove to Emile's office at Greenwich Plaza and parked in the visitor area. As I walked toward the building, I saw the younger of the two thugs who had been in my office, parked across the lot, sitting in a black Cadillac Escalade. I looked directly at him and nodded. He nodded back. I made a mental note of his license plate number and went inside.

The door to Emile's outer office was locked. I called the office number again, to see if I could hear anyone respond. Aside from the ringing there was nothing.

I went back the building's reception area and asked the receptionist if he'd seen Emile or Bev that day. He said neither had been around for a couple of weeks.

Chapter 13:

Five years later, there was still no sign of Emile or Bev.

In the immediate aftermath of their disappearance, the same day that the thugs came to my office, I drove to Emile's house and discovered that he'd sold it and moved away. The new owners had already been living there for a few weeks. I also learned that months earlier, Bev had let the lease on her apartment lapse and moved in with Emile. According to the neighbor, nothing about their departure seemed abnormal or abrupt. By that time Emile was in his early sixties and he told a couple of people that he was fed up with Connecticut winters and taxes and was heading south to Naples, Florida. His neighbors had the impression that Bev went with him.

After searching on my own for a month, I enlisted the help of a Greenwich police officer who I knew was a friend of Emile's, an affable guy named Mike Eastmure. I was able to convince Mike that the circumstances of their disappearance were questionable. He agreed to help.

Together we established that on September 10, 2012 they'd rented a mid-sized U Haul truck in nearby Stamford, Connecticut, in Bev's name. The truck had been returned seventeen days later, in Naples. If they were trying to disappear, they could have gone almost anywhere in the country and back in seventeen days. And in 2012, there were still plenty of manned tollbooths, so it would have been fairly easy for them to travel under the radar. Aside from dropping off the rental truck, we weren't able to find any evidence that they settled or even stayed in Naples. On September 11th, Emile purchased gas at a rest stop on I-95 north of Baltimore and again in Virginia, just off the same interstate. They spent the night of the 11th at a Holiday Inn Express in Petersburg, Virginia, twenty-five miles south of Richmond.

There wasn't another trace of them that we could find until September 27th when Bev turned the empty truck to a U Haul rental center in Naples.

That was it. We had no idea where they were or what happened to them.

With every other lead dried up and Eastmure's interest diminishing, I decided to approach Geordie Hendrie, the man who sent his henchmen to my office. We met at his golf club, Stanwich, arguably the best course in Connecticut. One of his henchmen met me in the parking lot and took me to him. He was sitting on the patio, having lunch.

Hendrie was about sixty and in decent shape. As we approached, he looked up from his lunch. He nodded at the chair across from him. As I sat, he dismissed his associate saying, "Thanks, Hank."

I extended my hand across the table.

"Thanks for seeing me, Mr. Hendrie."

Holding a section of a sandwich he waved off the handshake. "No problem. You said you want to talk to me about Coulon?"

"Yes. Do you have any idea where he is?"

He looked straight at me, trying to read me. "No."

"May I ask why you wanted to find him? Why you sent your men to see me?"

"No."

"Was he working for you?"

He looked at me like I was an idiot. "Fuck no. Why would I hire that jackass?"

He took a bite of his sandwich, a good-looking turkey club, and said, "I didn't let you come here to ask me questions."

He went back to chewing, waiting for me to respond.

"Okay, what do you want to know?"

"What did you do for him?"

I considered how I would answer. I figured he somehow knew we investigated him. "I helped him with his cases. Some individual stuff, but mostly with corporate clients, doing things like background checks and serving summonses."

"You're a hedge fund guy, right? You run a little fund?"

"Yes."

"Why would you work for Coulon? There can't be much money doing penny-ante shit like that."

"I think Emile did pretty well with it, but you're right, I didn't make much. I just enjoyed the work."

He smirked. "Coulon did better than pretty well, but it wasn't doing the shit you're talking about."

"What do you mean?"

He ignored my question. "I find it hard to believe that a guy like you, who makes a reasonable jack, would waste his time serving fucking summonses. Were you helping him with the other shit?"

Now we were getting somewhere. "What other shit?"

He just stared at me, again seeming to try to read me. "I had you checked out. I know your record and reputation. You're clean as a whistle, but I didn't know you were fucking stupid."

"What are you talking about?"

"The guy was a money-making machine. He was... Christ, didn't you know? Are you fucking blind?"

"A money-making machine? Doing what?"

He looked at me incredulously. "Seriously? He had you doing his leg work and you didn't even know it."

"What are you talking about?"

He just shook his head and nodded at Hank, who was at a table with another thug across the patio. Hank came over and stood next to me. I just sat there. "Please tell me what you're talking about."

He picked up his sandwich and looked at Hank. Hank put his hand on my shoulder. Now I was dismissed, apparently not worth any more of Hendrie's time. I stood and walked to my car, with Hank escorting me.

I got in and closed the door, but just sat there, trying to figure out what Hendrie had been talking about.

Hank knocked a knuckle on my window and nodded toward the gate. Once again, I was dismissed.

As I drove away, a knot developed in my stomach. It was a terrible feeling to know I'd been stupid and not know why.

It would take me another five years to figure it out.

Chapter 14:

In June of 2017, private equity billionaire Howard Rawlings announced that he was running for the US Senate. Like other people I'd investigated, I was always interested when I saw Rawlings in the news. And because he was my very first case, I guess I had a special interest in him. In the time since we'd caught him fooling around, his fortunes and reputation had continued to expand. As far as I knew, that reputation didn't include even a hint of his fondness for men.

Although Rawlings had been on my radar for almost twenty years, we'd never met. We didn't run in anywhere near the same circles. When I finally did meet him, the billionaire was trying to raise money from "wealthy" people like me. After decades of watching the shit show that is American politics, my feelings about the two primary political parties were somewhere between agnostic and outright atheist, but because of my curiosity about Rawlings, I went to his fundraiser.

The event was taking place at the Greenwich home of an elderly woman, a party dowager whose late husband held the seat Rawlings was after, albeit decades earlier. There were only thirty of us there, so the pressure to donate was going to be intense.

After twenty minutes of cocktails and chatter, our hostess asked for our attention. She explained that the candidate had arrived and on cue, he stepped into the room. To my great surprise he was accompanied by his wife Gina, the same wife who had employed Emile so many years ago. She was still beautiful.

After a not-too-brief introduction, Rawlings said a few words, but thankfully refrained from making a full speech. He said instead he'd rather talk with us individually, to hear our concerns and get to know us. Smooth bullshit.

At first he spoke with the bigger players in the room. He seemed to know who everyone was. His aides worked the rest of us.

I made my way to the makeshift bar and asked the bartender for a beer. Mrs. Rawlings appeared next to me.

She turned and smiled. "Hi. I'm Gina Rawlings."

She extended her hand. Even it was beautiful. I smiled back and shook her hand. "Hi. Phil Osgood."

"It's nice to meet you. Thank you for coming."

We made small talk for a minute or two and then she asked me what I did for a living. I considered my answer for a moment, longer than it usually takes to answer such a simple question and finally said, "A couple of things."

I had the sense that she knew exactly who everyone in the room was and what they did for a living, so I think my answer caught her by surprise.

She smiled her stunning smile. "What does that mean?"

"I run a fund. A small one by your husband's standards."

She nodded. Having been surrounded by finance guys for decades, most vastly less successful than her husband but many with larger egos, she was used to people like me.

"And the other thing?"

Her curiosity seemed genuine.

"I worked as a private detective."

As expected, that got her attention.

"You don't hear that every day."

No one else was paying attention to our conversation so I quietly added, "Actually I did some work for you, years ago."

That really caught her by surprise. She seemed confused, so I added, "I worked with Emile Coulon."

There was an instant of recognition in her eyes, but I didn't get anything else.

She smiled and said, "I'm sure glad you guys didn't find ..."

A firm hand grasped my shoulder and I turned to face its owner. Howard Rawlings extended his other hand. "Hi. I'm Howard Rawlings."

He lowered his voice and in a distinctly colder tone said, "What are you doing here?"

I was shocked by his brusqueness. "You invited me."

I looked from Howard to his wife. She seemed equally surprised by his tone, which confused me even more.

To try to diffuse things I extended my hand and said, "It's nice to meet you, Mr. Rawlings."

He stared at me and I guess for the sake of appearances, shook my hand. After an awkward silence he said, "Excuse us. There's someone I want Gina to meet." He gently touched his wife's elbow. As they stepped away he added, "I'd like to talk with you sometime though. I'll be in touch."

"Sure."

I stood there trying to figure out what had happened.

Rawlings and his wife were accompanied by an aide. She must have told him my name and given him some background information. He'd have been told I managed a fund, but the aide wouldn't have known I'd also worked with Coulon years earlier. From the perspective of his staff, I was just another potential donor at one of what must have been dozens of fundraisers he attended. But it was apparent that Rawlings did know. As soon as he saw someone associated with Coulon, someone who might know his secret, he panicked.

Even though the investigation had taken place twenty years ago, and he and his wife had apparently managed some sort of marital resolution, he was running as a conservative Republican. Any hint of his bisexuality would crush his candidacy.

As her husband led her away Mrs. Rawlings looked over her shoulder at me. She seemed disturbed, but I couldn't tell if she was confused or angry.

The event lasted for another hour and I didn't get another chance to talk with either Rawlings or his wife. I did "get" to donate $250 to his campaign. Not anywhere near what his staff was looking for but enough to get me out the door.

As I drove home, I replayed the conversation with Gina Rawlings in my mind. Before her husband stopped her she'd said, "I'm glad you guys didn't find..." Glad about not finding what? Was her husband doing something worse than sleeping with men?

And why was Howard so upset? Did he think I was there to use the information I had on him for my advantage? That I might blackmail him?

That made sense. And it fit with Gina Rawlings' reaction. She seemed genuinely surprised when I told her I worked with Emile.

I considered trying to meet with Rawlings, to diffuse his fears. But I had no idea how much Mrs. Rawlings had told her husband about Emile's investigation. She'd obviously been willing to look beyond his infidelity. What right did I have to mettle in their business? If Rawlings initiated contact with me, I'd meet him. But I wouldn't set up a meeting myself.

The next morning as I was sitting at my desk reading the paper, my phone rang. The display said, "Private Caller." I answered it.

"Mr. Osgood?" It was a woman's voice. "This is Gina Rawlings."

"Hi, Mrs. Rawlings."

"Hi." She paused. "I was wondering if I could talk with you?"

"Of course. But I can assure you..."

She cut me off. "Let's meet in person."

Forty-five minutes later we met in a parking lot and walked along a sidewalk in a very public, very open park.

"Thank you for meeting with me."

"Of course."

We walked for a minute as she appeared to consider how to start. "Mr. Osgood, I'm a little confused about last night."

"I feel badly about last night, Mrs. Rawlings."

"Why?"

"I don't want you to think I would ever use the information Emile and I found about your husband for anything, well for anything at all. I can assure you I've never mentioned it to anyone and never will."

She stopped walking and turned to face me. "What information?"

Now I was confused. Why would she want me to describe his affair? To see if I really knew? Tentatively I said, "The information Emile gave you."

"What are you talking about?"

Even though we were alone I lowered my voice. "The report Emile Coulon gave to you after you hired him back in '98."

She looked even more confused. "I don't understand."

"Didn't Emile Coulon give you a report on your husband's – his activities?"

"He told me he couldn't find anything."

Now I was confused and in a very awkward position.

When I didn't say anything, she went on. "You said you and Emile found something. What did you find?"

What a fucking mess I'd gotten myself into. "It's not my place to tell you."

"What do you mean it's not your place. That ship has sailed. What did you find?"

"Ethically, I can't tell you. It's up to Emile."

"I tried to call him this morning, but there wasn't a listing for him. Not for his business or his residence."

"I know. He's gone."

She didn't understand the full import of him being gone, but probably wouldn't have cared anyway.

"Then you're going to have to tell me."

"I can't. It's not right for me to. I don't know all the facts."

We argued for a few more minutes, but didn't get anywhere. Part of me wanted to tell her, but I knew I couldn't. What right did I have to ruin Rawlings' marriage or his reputation?

When we parted, she was understandably furious with me, but I felt that was better than upending her life.

Three hours later my phone rang again. This time it was Howard Rawlings.

"What the fuck did you tell my wife?"

"I didn't tell her anything,"

"I'm parked downstairs, black Suburban. Get your fucking ass down here."

He hung up. I walked down the hall to the conference room at the front of our building, overlooking the street. Rawlings' Suburban was parked across the street.

I walked back down the hall past my office to the steps leading downstairs. Then I thought better of it and went back to my office and wrote a note on a post-it. *Meeting with Howard Rawlings in his black Suburban. 6/21/17, 1:15pm on Havermeyer Road.* I put it on my desk, under a pile of papers.

I walked back down the steps and then outside. I stopped on my side of Havermeyer. The driver's side front window of the Suburban went down. Rawlings nodded to me. I crossed the street and got in the front passenger seat. There was no one else in the car.

He closed his window and pulled out.

"What the fuck are you doing?"

"Nothing. I'm sorry. I didn't mean to upset your wife."

"Fuck you."

"I can understand why you're upset."

The normally composed man was livid. "Fuck off. It's bad enough that fucking Coulon blackmailed me. Now you're trying to get your piece too?"

And just like that, everything fell into place. God. I was stupid.

Emile blackmailed Rawlings.

I realized Rawlings was yelling at me.

"Mr. Rawlings, I'm sorry."

A traffic cop on Greenwich Avenue directed us to come forward and Rawlings turned left and drove down the hill, under the train bridge at the bottom of the avenue, right by the office building where Emile and I used to work.

"What do you want?"

"Nothing."

"Nothing?"

"I didn't know Emile was blackmailing you."

"Bullshit."

"I didn't."

"Then you're an idiot." He paused. "Why did you confront my wife?"

"I didn't confront her."

"Why did you even bring up the investigation if you didn't want anything?"

"Coulon's been missing for years. Almost five years. I've been trying to find him. When I see former clients, I try to discreetly ask if they've heard from him."

"Discreetly? At a fucking fundraiser?"

"Believe me, I didn't think it would be that big of a deal. I'm just trying to find a friend."

"A friend? The guy's a fucking crook." He paused again. "Do you really expect me to believe that you didn't know he was blackmailing me?"

I looked directly at him. We were on a quiet tree lined street near the Bruce Museum, not far from where I had walked with his wife a few hours earlier. He pulled over and parked.

"I had no idea."

Rawlings looked at me, trying to size me up. I had a hard time believing that he wasn't reaching the same conclusion Hendrie had reached five years earlier.

"Now that you know, what do you want?"

"I don't want anything."

That wasn't really true. I did want information, but the most important thing was to convince him that I didn't want to do anything to hurt him or his family.

"I find that very hard to believe."

"Look Mr. Rawlings, I'm an honest man. I've never stolen anything. I worked with Coulon because I enjoyed the work." I paused and then added, "And I liked him. But once I knew he was less than honest I stopped working with him."

"So you knew he was a blackmailer."

"No. I thought he was cutting corners and at the end that he was dealing with unscrupulous people. Once I learned that, I stopped working with him. I had no idea he was blackmailing you."

"And now that you know?"

"I don't know." My mind raced. "Do you know he's been missing? Since 2012?"

He considered his answer, then shrugged. I couldn't tell if he'd seen Emile since then or not.

"I don't know how to convince you that I'm honest Mr. Rawlings, but I can promise you that I don't want any money from you and I certainly won't be telling your wife or the media anything about you."

Adding the media to the conversation was a mistake on my part. He glared at me.

"Do you know how easy it would be for me to ruin your little fund?"

I held his gaze.

"I do. I'm sure it would be very easy for you."

We sat there, staring at each other, knowing we could each ruin the other's life. The difference was that I knew I wouldn't do it.

"I have no interest and nothing to gain from hurting you or Mrs. Rawlings."

He considered what I said.

"And as easily as I could crush you, I could make you a star. I could double the size of your fund tomorrow. And if I put $50 million in, do you know how many other investors would follow?"

Those were words I had hoped to hear from a major player for twenty years. But I didn't want his money. Not like that.

"Please don't. Really. I don't want anything from you. And you don't owe me anything. You don't have to pay me to keep me quiet."

"How do I know I can trust you?"

"I don't know how I can prove it to you. But I think of it this way. Emile paid me to do some work for him. I did the work. You or your wife paid him for the results of our work. It was Emile's information to give to his client, Mrs. Rawlings. I'm sorry he exploited you with that information, but I didn't and I won't. And I won't tell your wife or anyone else. It's not my information to disclose."

We sat there for a minute and then he said, "Get out."

Chapter 15:

I'd helped a blackmailer. I could go to jail.

For the next few days I did little other than process that ugly reality. It was clear that in addition to blackmailing Rawlings, Coulon had also probably tried to blackmail Geordie Hendrie and Kim Campbell, the lawyer at Dewey, Grant & Howe, or perhaps one of his clients. I had no idea how many other clients he'd extorted money from or how often I'd been the one who found the information he'd used for his blackmail.

Was the irate husband who beat him up reacting to blackmail? Was he blackmailing his client in Chicago, if that client even existed? Had he opened the Chicago office to put some distance between him and the people he was blackmailing?

I thought about the money. If he charged Mrs. Rawlings her full fees and expenses, maybe he'd have made $5,000. But if he went to Mr. Rawlings, a billionaire with political ambitions and said give me money or face a likely divorce and a ruined reputation, he could have demanded so much more. Even if the Rawlings had a prenup for $5 to $10 million, paying off Emile would be much cheaper. And if there wasn't a prenup, a divorce would cost him half of everything. Emile could have demanded exorbitant sums.

And if he had been blackmailing people as far back as 1998, when we'd worked on the Rawlings case, he may have tapped dozens of people, maybe more. It was amazing Emile and Bev weren't in jail. Hell, it was hard to believe I wasn't. No wonder they went into hiding.

I considered my options and thought about going to the police. Detective Mike Eastmure, the Greenwich cop who'd opened the investigation into Emile and Bev's disappearance, had only taken a perfunctory look. I could talk to him about it, but I wasn't sure he'd care. As far as I knew, no one had seen

Emile or Bev since 2012. If anyone was going to press charges with regard to the blackmail, surely they already would have.

What if I did go to the police? If there was any publicity even suggesting I was involved in a blackmail scheme or anything illegal, most of my fund clients would be gone in an instant. Then what would I do?

But if I didn't inform the police, wouldn't I be breaking the law? That could come back and really bite me in the ass. Christ, I didn't want the stress of living with that.

In the end I decided to talk with Eastmure.

We met that evening at about 6:30 in a bar at the bottom of Greenwich Avenue. After we exchanged the usual pleasantries, I got to the point.

"Emile Coulon was blackmailing his clients. Our clients. As it turns out he may have used, no, he did use information I got for him to blackmail at least one of the people we were investigating. I had no knowledge of any of this. The incident I'm talking about took place in 1998. I learned about the blackmail four days ago from that person, the man he was blackmailing."

"Holy shit, Phil."

"I know. I didn't know, Mike. I had no idea."

He just stared at me, trying to process everything he heard. "Who did he blackmail?"

"I can't say. Or at least I'm not going to say, unless I'm legally obligated to do it."

"Then why are you telling me? How am I supposed to help if I don't know where to start?"

"I don't know. But if the blackmailed person wanted you to know, he could tell you."

"You say this all happened in '98? Nineteen years ago?"

"The investigation took place then. I'm not sure when the blackmail occurred. For all I know it could still be going on."

"Has Coulon surfaced?"

"I don't think so. So far as I know, the last time anyone saw him or Bev was in 2012, when she turned in the rented moving truck."

"Did you ask the guy when the last time Coulon demanded money from him was? Or whether it was an ongoing thing?"

"I didn't ask him anything about the specifics. To be honest I was trying to convince him I wasn't part of the original blackmail and that I wasn't trying to start my own extortion plan."

"Shit. Did he believe you?"

"I don't know."

Mike thought for a minute then asked, "So what do you want me to do with this information?"

"I don't know. But it sheds new light on why they disappeared."

"What are you saying?"

"Well, maybe they're hiding or maybe –" I paused.

"Maybe what?"

"Maybe they're dead."

Chapter 16:

I decided to take another look at everything I knew about Emile and Bev's activities. The fact that they were blackmailers, or at least that Emile was, gave me an entirely new perspective on trying to find them.

I made a list of the clients I'd worked with. Emile had requested that I not keep written records of work related to his clients and I had always respected that. But I did have calendar entries of meetings, so my list of names was fairly comprehensive. Once I completed the list, I wrote down as much detail as I could remember about the work we did for each client. Then I went down the list, name by name, and tried to evaluate the details of the investigations to see if it was the sort of thing that could be used for blackmail.

Every infidelity case had blackmail potential. During the period from '98 through 2010, I worked on thirty-eight cases in which we found evidence of infidelity. I examined each case and did what I could to ascertain the wealth of the parties. I figured that, given the risks associated with blackmail, Emile would focus on cases with the biggest potential payoffs.

A few of the clients, people like Rawlings, were so wealthy that a simple Google search could establish that they had enough money to be tempting to Emile. With others I looked at their jobs to get a sense of their wealth. And with some, I simply drove by their homes.

Then I checked to see if the couple was divorced. I figured that if a couple did divorce and it happened within a year or two of our investigation, there was a good chance that Emile had told the actual client about the infidelity and the couple hadn't been blackmailed or wasn't willing to be.

Admittedly that was a lot of fuzzy logic, but I had to shorten the list somehow.

I also looked at the nature of infidelity. If the activity was potentially embarrassing, he or she might be more susceptible to extortion. For example, over the years a few clients had been involved in some pretty strange sexual activities. While some people might find that embarrassing and others might not, I considered those with unusual sexual appetites to be more likely to have been targeted by Coulon and moved them up the list.

At the end of that process I had ten infidelity-related clients who Emile might have viewed as attractive blackmail candidates.

Then I went through Emile's corporate clients, again trying to find people he might have targeted.

Dewey, Grant & Howe, the law firm who'd summarily fired me and had me escorted from their offices, was on the top of that list. I figured Emile must have tried to blackmail them or one of their clients. We were terminated in June of 2010, so I focused on investigations we'd done for Dewey in the prior twelve months. When I looked at the list of Dewey's clients we'd investigated, one name stood out: Southwestern County Bancorp (SWCB).

SWCB was a small but growing bank in Fairfield County, Connecticut. The bank was formed by a group of retired traders in 2001. In 2010, a larger regional bank was considering acquiring Southwestern. Dewey hired Emile to look into the bank's operations. Campbell said they had finance guys sifting through the numbers and didn't want to duplicate that effort. He wanted Emile to look at Southwestern from the ground level to see if we could find anything irregular. Emile handed the investigation over to me.

When I was a kid my grandfather owned a small consumer loan company in western Pennsylvania. He had a man he trusted, Jay Anderson, manage the company for him. At one point, after Jay had been running the company for almost twenty years, my grandfather decided to sell it to a national loan company.

Before the national company's accountants got their hands on the company's books, Jay told my grandfather that he'd been stealing from him. For years Jay had been making loans to fictitious customers and pocketing the money himself. If he took out a $3,000 loan for an imaginary client, he would use some of the money to keep the loan current and pocket the rest. A month or two before the loan came due, he would create another false client and take out a larger loan to pay off the maturing loan, pocket some of the new money and start all over again. The scheme was problematic because he always needed bigger loans to keep it afloat.

At any rate, Anderson knew he would get caught when the new owners looked into the loans, so rather than surely facing the authorities, he came clean to my grandfather.

I never forgot the lesson. When we were looking at SWCB for Dewey, I asked to see a list of loans and the associated properties. I took the list and started knocking on doors, to make sure the names on the loans were the same as the names on the properties and that they were legitimate.

After just two days of knocking, before I'd found any discrepancies, the manager of one of Southwestern's bigger branches asked for a meeting. He explained that one of the owners, Justin Graber, was secretly paying him to make loans to fictitious customers. It was Jay Anderson all over again.

After the meeting I called Emile and explained the situation. Emile said he'd handle it.

A week or two later he told me that he met with the lawyers from Dewey and told them about Graber's illegal loans. He said that for the sake of the bank and their own reputations, Graber and SWCB's other owners paid off the loans themselves. He said he wasn't sure what would happen after that. As with everything we did, we weren't to speak a word of it.

And that was that. The merger talks ended and so did our investigation. I remember how proud I was of our diligent work.

Knowing what I now know, I assume Emile went straight to Graber and tried to blackmail him. And that seemed to have worked – for a few months. Then it must have come out, probably in early June, in advance of Campbell firing us on the 14th.

I tried to talk to Campbell to get to the bottom of it, but in spite of countless efforts including approaching him on the street, I couldn't get him to talk to me.

Chapter 17:

After SWCB, I moved on to other names on my list.

Rather than talking to the people who'd actually hired us, I contacted the people we'd been hired to investigate, the ones who had presumably committed the blackmailable act. I talked to adulterers, abusers, bank robbers, conmen, dope fiends, perverts, pedophiles, crooks, embezzlers, mother-rapers, father-rapers and even a litterer. But every time I met one of them, I got pretty much the same response I did from Rawlings. Every person I approached knew I knew his or her transgression, and some assumed that like Emile, I wanted money for my silence. They weren't exactly helpful.

I tried to convince them that I didn't want anything other than information about Emile. But frankly, they couldn't care less about him. His disappearance was probably viewed as a relief. I'm sure many of them hoped he was dead.

I didn't know if Emile was hiding somewhere, living off his blackmail money, or if he was dead. His potential death had serious implications. Instead of just questioning people he might have blackmailed, I might have been questioning a murderer.

Nonetheless, I kept digging. Along with Rawlings and Graber, several other former clients made my short list.

One was a doctor from Rye, New York named Rahm Patel. Emile and I investigated Patel in 2007. He was an internist with an expanding practice who wanted to lease an entire building from a real estate investment company. The company's own due-diligence team felt something wasn't quite right about Patel. They hired Emile to check him out before agreeing to lease him the building and share the cost of reconfiguring it to the doctor's specifications.

As with any potential lessee, Patel had provided the landlord with his practice's financials for the prior three years.

They were impressive – too impressive. The landlord had over a half a billion dollars of real estate holdings in affluent communities around ~~the~~ New York City and had a pretty good sense of doctors' earning potential. Patel's numbers were outlandishly high.

We investigated him but, because of doctor-patient confidentiality, couldn't get patient names for interviews.

After repeated prodding, Patel did give us the name of his bookkeeper, a man who operated a one-man firm north of Albany. Patel said that while he was a long way away, he was skilled in navigating the complexities of dealing with insurance companies and Medicare and Medicaid. We talked with the bookkeeper, who had been working with Patel for two years. He provided us with detailed revenue and expense statements, but only in the aggregate. Without patient names or information on the number of patients or average number of visits per patient, we couldn't really understand his business. We weren't getting anywhere.

Patel had been practicing in the area since 1991 and obviously had bookkeepers prior to the Albany guy. But by the time we got around to looking for his previous bookkeepers, we had pretty much worn out our welcome with the doctor. Our client, the real estate company, felt we had done our due diligence and was considering just going with him. But I asked Emile to tell them something seemed a little off and to ask for a few more days. The client agreed but made it clear they didn't want us to sour the deal, so we had to tread carefully.

Rather than risking bothering Patel again, I talked to several doctors I knew, and asked them to recommend bookkeepers. I got a list of a dozen or so and checked them out.

The fourth one I called had worked with Patel. I asked her some questions about him and she clammed up. I decided to visit her at her office in Port Chester, New York.

When I showed up, she was surprised but agreed to talk with me. She operated a one-woman firm and her office looked a lot like some I had rented over the years, a basic cube with a desk, three chairs, a credenza and some file cabinets.

I had a sense that she didn't like Patel so I didn't think she would call him about our visit and wasn't too worried about my questions getting back to him and ruffling his feathers. I told her the truth about my assignment and my gut feeling about the doctor. She said my instincts were accurate and that she'd only kept Patel's books for three years. She said she quit working for him because she felt uncomfortable with his numbers.

She reluctantly admitted that she suspected he was committing Medicare fraud by claiming to have had numerous visits with clients he actually only met once or twice. She had access to the patients' names and said that she had called one patient who Patel had billed for eleven visits. The patient said he had only been to see the doctor two or three times.

Patel was bilking the federal government. I asked if she had reported it and she nervously said she hadn't. None of the other bookkeepers were as forthcoming, but a second acknowledged that he stopped working for Patel because he wasn't comfortable with the doctor's billings.

I'd reported my findings to Emile and he told me he'd inform the client. I assumed our client walked away from the deal and that was the end of it. I looked up Patel's current address. It was 47 Baily Street in Rye. He had moved into our client's building and was still there. Emile must not have reported our findings to the client and probably blackmailed Patel.

That evening I visited Patel, catching him as he walked from his office to his car.

"Dr. Patel?"

Patel was about fifty-five, well dressed and approaching a 7 series BMW. He looked a little irritated that I approached him after his office hours. He gave me a polite but obviously insincere smile.

"My name is Phil Osgood."

There was no apparent recognition of my name, which wasn't surprising. He continued toward his car.

"I used to work with Emile Coulon."

That wiped the smug smile from his face. He turned and said, "Fuck off."

"I beg your pardon?"

"You heard me. Fuck the hell off."

"I want to talk to you about Coulon."

"I don't want to talk to you or him. And if you know what's good for you, you'll walk away. Now."

He got into his car and drove off.

I put Patel on my short list.

Chapter 18:

The next person I investigated was a man named Steve Walker. Walker's wife hired Emile in 2010 because they were getting divorced and she was convinced that her husband was significantly understating the value of his business, Royal Foods Company (RFC).

Walker purchased Royal Foods from his uncle in 1987. At that time RFC was a smallish holding company with seven diners in southwestern Connecticut. By 2010, when we were hired, Walker had grown it into a regional powerhouse that owned one hundred and ninety-one restaurants from Maryland to Maine.

Royal Foods was privately held so finding its real value was difficult. We had the reports Walker supplied to his wife's divorce attorney, but those were the reports that caused Mrs. Walker to think her husband was understating the company's value. And we had tax returns. The income in the tax returns was consistent with the numbers in the RFC reports.

Most of RFC's revenue came from the restaurants. Each restaurant was owned by up to three LLCs, and each LLC owned a piece of anywhere from twenty to sixty of RFC's restaurants. Royal Foods owned a minority stake in all of the LLCs, but the legal structure was so complex that it was difficult to trace the majority owners. They were all registered offshore in places like the Grand Caymans and Monserrat – known tax havens. It seemed possible that Walker was hiding revenue and avoiding taxes. But the restaurants themselves did incredibly well. They were cash-generating machines.

I checked the reports for restaurants near me. I had eaten at three of them and one was in my town, New Canaan. It was a Chinese restaurant called Szechuan Garden. The food there was terrible. Most of the people I knew ate at the other Chinese restaurant in town, Ching's Table.

As far as Chinese food in New Canaan was concerned, I was something of an expert. From the time my first son was born, Jenny and I ordered Chinese food and rented a movie almost every Friday night. As our family grew so did the size of our order. By the time my boys were all in school, the owner of Ching's Table knew me by my first name and often thanked me at Christmas time, telling me that I'd been her best customer that year.

I decided to do an experiment, using Ching's Table and Szechuan Garden as guinea pigs.

Ching's Table was open seven days a week and offered both take out and eat in. One Friday I parked outside Ching's Table and watched. The cash register was right by the door so I could watch every time someone paid. From 11am until they closed at 10pm, ninety-three people picked up take out and thirty-two parties had eaten there. The average take-out bill for my family of six was about $80. If each customer's bill was as big as mine, and if all of the eat-in customers spent another $50 on beverages, Ching's Table revenue that Friday would have been $11,600.

The next day, a Saturday, I did the same thing outside of Walker's restaurant, Szechuan Garden. They had forty-one take-out customers and twenty-six eat-in parties. Using the same math, Szechuan took in $6,600.

If the restaurants did those levels of business on every Friday, Saturday and Sunday, and half that each of the other weekdays and both were open fifty-one weeks a year, their annual revenues would have been $2,958,000 and $1,683,000 respectively.

My first thought was that I should open a Chinese restaurant.

I compared my very hypothetical numbers with the reports Mrs. Walker and her attorney provided. Restaurants take in large portions of their revenues in cash and they're notorious for hiding income. I expected Szechuan's revenues to come in well below my $1.7 million estimate. The restaurant had revenues of $3.1 million in 2008 and $3.7 million in 2009.

It made no sense.

I googled US restaurant profit margins and found they averaged between 10% and 15%. Szechuan Garden's profit margins were 11% in 2008 and 13% in 2009.

If they were padding revenues, they were also padding expenses.

I drove to RFC restaurants in five other states and used the same questionable process to estimate their revenues. Every time the revenues in RFC's reports significantly exceeded my estimates. Every single time.

RFC's restaurants were generating a lot of income, but I couldn't figure out how.

We decided Emile should talk with Mrs. Walker to see if she knew. But that required some finesse. She thought the value of the business was being understated but wouldn't want to disclose anything that would undermine or implicate the business and reduce her take.

Emile had met her twice before and said she loathed her husband. He thought that if he played on that, talking about what an amazing businessman Walker must be to run his restaurants so well, she might get angry and unintentionally give us some hint of where to look.

The Machiavellian son-of-a-bitch was right. When they met, Emile said he went on and on about how smart her husband was and that in no time, Mrs. Walker cracked. She said her husband was nothing more than an errand boy for a man named Geordie Hendrie, who was the brains behind everything.

At that point neither Emile nor I knew Hendrie, but because of his mob ties, we knew who he was. With a little digging I discovered that he owned two apparently legitimate businesses; a commercial real estate company called Granite Holdings which owned retail properties and office buildings throughout New York's northern suburbs and a good-sized regional trucking company, Hendrie Trucking. The trucking company was the first connection I found between Hendrie and Walker. Royal Foods used Hendrie Trucking to move its restaurant supplies.

There had to be more. I dug deeper.

When Walker purchased Royal Foods from his uncle in 1987, he sold three of the original seven dinners and used the proceeds to open a high-end seafood restaurant in Westport, Connecticut.

That didn't go well. It closed just two years later. The restaurant remained closed for nine months then reopened in 1991. The second time it succeeded.

It struck me as odd that he reopened the same restaurant. I figured I'd talk to the landlord to see if Walker had tried to get out of his lease. It turned out the landlord was Geordie Hendrie's Granite Holdings. A second connection.

After the reopened seafood restaurant succeeded, Walker never looked back. He started acquiring more restaurants: two in 1994, five in 1995 and so on to his 2010 total of one hundred ninety-one. Aside from the four remaining original diners, which Walker owned outright, the other restaurants all had the similar and complex legal structures; Royal owned between 10% and 20% and a combination of LLCs owned the rest.

RFC issued K-1s to each LLC, so I at least had a starting point to track down the underlying ownership. I randomly picked a mid-sized LLC, Ridley Partners. Ridley was based in George Town, Grand Cayman. It was owned by two LLCs, one based in Geneva, Switzerland and the other in Monserrat. Three layers later, I discovered Appleby Partners, based in Bermuda. Appleby was owned by Lakefield Holdings, an LLC based in Delaware owned by one Geordie Hendrie, of Greenwich, Connecticut.

I traced the layers behind three additional LLC's that cumulatively owned majority shares in Walker's restaurants. They all eventually led to Hendrie.

Emile and I discussed it at length. We were only speculating, but we figured that when Walker's original Westport restaurant went under back in 1991, Hendrie, his landlord, made him an offer to stay in business, *an offer he couldn't refuse.* We speculated that Hendrie became Walker's partner to use RFC's restaurants to launder money from his illegal businesses. We surmised that after the scheme worked for a couple of years in Westport, Hendrie decided to expand on a good thing, and started acquiring more restaurants to clean their money. According to their tax filings in 2009 Royal Foods Company had revenues of $362.9 million. In my sample of six restaurants, it appeared that they were placing as much or more money than the restaurants were actually bringing in. If half of Royal's revenues came from legitimate operations, Hendrie and Walker were laundering over $180 million dollars a year.

This was beyond the scope of anything we'd come across in the past. I felt that we had to go to the authorities. Emile disagreed, saying it was too risky. But I continued to insist and eventually he said he'd discuss it with an FBI agent he knew.

A week or two later he said his friend at the FBI was understandably vague but led him to believe that the FBI was aware of everything we surmised and that for our own safety we should leave it alone. Emile said he told Mrs. Walker we couldn't find anything. And that was the last I heard of it.

I was surprised that Emile risked blackmailing someone like Walker, who was connected to someone like Hendrie. But since Hendrie came looking for him, he must have. Hendrie didn't come to my office until 2012 even though we did our RFC work in 2010. It apparently took Emile a year or two to get up the nerve to go after Walker's potentially huge payout. Or maybe it was because, since I stopped working for him in 2010, he hadn't found another idiot to do his legwork and his pipeline had gone dry.

Chapter 19:

After months of research, I decided to step back and evaluate what I knew. First, I had no doubt that Emile was a crook. He had probably blackmailed or attempted to blackmail dozens of people. I knew nothing about whether he blackmailed each person once or multiple times, but my guess was that like most blackmailers, he kept going back. And, in spite of my desire to believe otherwise, it seemed Bev was helping him.

They'd been scamming clients since at least 1998 when Emile blackmailed Rawlings, and it seemed likely that they'd kept doing it until June of 2012 when they disappeared. Whether they disappeared of their own free will or were disposed of by someone they blackmailed, I didn't know.

Some of the people Emile and Bev blackmailed had enough to lose and seemed coldblooded enough to have actually killed them. Walker and Hendrie were at the top of that list. Graber the corrupt banker and Patel the crooked doctor also had motive. If Emile outed them, they'd have been ruined and probably imprisoned. Howard Rawlings had motive too.

The other probable blackmail victims I knew about undoubtedly had issues with Emile, but none were as menacing or had as much to lose as those five. And I didn't delude myself to believe my list was comprehensive. There were potentially dozens I knew nothing about.

One thing was certain. I had stirred the pot. There were a lot of people who viewed me as either another potential blackmailer or a person who knew their secret. Either way, I was in a dangerous position.

When I look back on it, I sometimes wish I had gone to the authorities and left it at that.

But I didn't. I wanted to get to the bottom of it, to find out what happened to my friend, who turned out not to have been much of a friend. Maybe I just wanted to confront him and say, 'Fuck you too, Emile. I figured you out.'

Chapter 20:

As it turned out, I never got a chance. In April of 2018 a construction crew found two bodies buried on a small island on Lake Rosseau in Ontario, Canada.

Lake Rosseau is in Muskoka, a beautiful lake district about two hours north of Toronto. I grew up in Toronto and went to junior high and high school there. One of my best friends from those years, a man named Andrew Allen, owned a small island on Rosseau. He and his wife Laura bought it from his uncle's estate. A year or two after they bought it, they tore down the old cottage and built a new one. In the process, they had to dig up and replace the old septic system to bring it up to code. On the second day of digging, workers discovered the bodies.

As a kid, I'd spent a lot of time on that island. Back then Andy's Uncle Tim owned it. Tim was an amazing host and even decades after I'd moved from Toronto, he'd invite Jenny and the boys and me up to visit. Typically, we went to spend time with him either during the summer or for Canadian Thanksgiving in October, but sometimes if he knew he was going to be traveling for a week or two, he'd invite us to use the cottage on our own.

We stayed there without Tim exactly once: in October of 2012, a month after Emile and Bev disappeared and a week after Hendrie's thugs visited me in my office.-

The second I heard that two bodies had been discovered on that island, I knew that Emile and Bev were dead and that the bodies were theirs.

Even though they'd used me and made a fool out of me, I never wanted them dead, especially not Bev. For years I'd feared the worst but sort of hoped for the best. I liked to imagine they were living on some foreign beach, old rogues who'd outsmarted me and blackmailed a bunch of rich people. But there was more to it. I wanted to find them myself, to confront Emile, to win. I was devastated.

I was also terrified.

Whoever killed Emile and Bev must have known I stayed there and set me up. I'd have bet a year's earnings that the killer buried them on Tim's island shortly after my family and I left. He probably assumed that the bodies would never be discovered. But he knew that if they were discovered and eventually identified, I'd become the prime suspect.

And that was only a part of my problems. Because of my investigation, many of Emile's blackmail victims now knew that I knew their secrets. If the bodies were identified as Bev and Emile, and if it became public that I was the primary suspect in their murders, sooner or later the blackmail victims would realize that, if implicated, I would talk. And if I talked, the information they'd paid to keep secret would come out.

I was fucked six ways to Sunday.

Chapter 21:

Before any of that happened, before I became a murder suspect and while I was still free and anonymous, I had to figure out who set me up.

I swapped cars with my brother-in-law, who lived in Larchmont, New York and headed north. If things got hairy in Ontario, I figured his New York plates would draw less attention than my Connecticut ones and buy me a little time. But I wasn't kidding myself. If the Canadian authorities tied my name to the bodies, they would check with their own customs and immigration department and quickly discover that I was in the country. But for the time being, I was just another tourist.

As I drove, I tried to piece everything together. Neither Emile nor Bev knew Tim or his nephew, Andy. But they did know about the island. Tim had a world-class collection of restored antique mahogany boats and after one of our visits, I'd shown Bev and Emile pictures of the boats and Tim's cottage.

If Emile and Bev wanted to hide during the off season, the island would have provided good cover. During the winter months Muskoka is a wickedly cold and sometimes bleak place. Most of the region's cottages are only built for summer use. They lack adequate heating and insulation to make them viable winter homes. Consequently, the vast majority of the cottages on and around the lakes are closed and vacant from November until April. Emile and Bev's killer may have followed them and used the winter cover – to murder and bury them. Or maybe someone who knew that I visited there wanted to frame me for their murders and somehow lured them to the island.

It seemed clear that when Bev and Emile left Greenwich back in 2012, their intent had been to disappear. Emile told his neighbors that they were moving to Naples, Florida. And, as Detective Mike Eastmure of the Greenwich police and I discovered six years earlier, they left a false trail to Naples. On September 10th of 2012 they rented a truck in Connecticut. On the 11th they paid for food, gas and a hotel room in Virginia using one of Emile's credit cards. Then there was no sign of them until Bev returned the truck in Naples two weeks later.

During those two weeks, they could have set up a new residence using new identities almost anywhere. If they paid cash for gas and food and stayed in cheap motels, they could have easily travelled without registering on the digital grid. And all these years later, even if some gas station or motel or restaurant's video surveillance system had caught them on tape, any records would be long gone.

Until the bodies turned up in Muskoka, I thought they had disappeared successfully. There hadn't been a single sign of them. Not one in six years.

But they hadn't gone into hiding. They were dead. Dead and buried on Tim's island.

Back in 2012, just three weeks after Bev returned the truck in Naples, I'd driven my family to Tim's cottage. It's possible that the killer followed us, hoping we'd lead him to Emile. Or he could have been following me to kill me too, since he probably believed I was a part of the blackmail team. Either way, the killer had to have been there that week. How else would he have known about the island? Unless Emile and Bev led him there.

I couldn't begin to put it all together. Why would they go there?

Had it all happened right after we'd left? I was pretty sure the cottage was empty. Tim had offered it to me for two weeks, but we'd only been able to stay for five days.

The lake was still busy in October, but the island was secluded. The killer could have easily buried them at night. By

December the ground would be too frozen to dig up. It seemed likely that they were either buried late that fall or in another off-season, in an October or November between 2013 and 2018, when they were found.

Would they have been killed on the island? Or at least in Canada? Transporting bodies across the Canadian border would have been incredibly risky. Did that mean it had to be Hendrie? Hendrie Trucking did do business in Canada. Would he have had the ability to hide two bodies in his trucks? But why take the risk?

No. They must have been killed in Canada.

The whole thing seemed crazy. Why go to all of the trouble of somehow luring them to Canada to kill them and frame me? It would have been much easier to kill them in Connecticut or Chicago. And it would have been a hell of a lot easier to kill me than to frame me.

Something wasn't right.

After twelve hours of driving, I finally made it to Port Carling, the town nearest to the Allen's island. My brain was fried and I was exhausted, but I didn't want to risk staying too close. I drove for another forty minutes and found a small motel near Huntsville.

The next morning, I got up early, went for a run, had breakfast, then drove back to Port Carling.

Ideally, I'd have rented a boat, but I couldn't do that without providing identification. Instead, I decided to hire a boat taxi to take me around the lake. Tim's cottage was the second island out the river from Port Carling, so we'd pretty much have to pass it. I figured I'd casually ask the driver about the bodies and have him drive me around the island. But when I walked down toward the lake, a TV crew was on the dock, interviewing a local. I didn't want any part of that. I turned and headed back to my car.

I thought about who else I knew on the lake. Another high school friend, Sandy Logie, had a cottage that wasn't far from Andy's. The cottage was on the mainland and Sandy had a boat: a little fiberglass outboard.

From memory I drove to Sandy's place. It was nicely rustic and I doubted it had an alarm system. It wouldn't have been too hard to break in, but Sandy was a good friend; I didn't want to damage his house or steal his boat. I decided I'd find a payphone, call him and call in my trades. It was a gorgeous, sunny spring morning, so I sat on his dock for an hour and complied the trades on my laptop. Then I drove to the nearest public place, a resort hotel called Windemere and phoned Sandy.

After we exchanged the usual pleasantries, I bluntly got to the point of my call.

"Sandy, I don't really want to go into any detail, but I'm up in Muskoka and need a boat. I was wondering if I could borrow yours for a day or two?"

"Sure. We're coming up on Friday night, I can take you out on Saturday. You can stay with us if you want."

"Actually, I need it today. Now."

"Why? What's up?"

I considered my answer for a moment.

"The less I tell you the better."

He started to laugh. "What are you talking about?"

"It's better if I don't tell you."

He stopped laughing. "What's going on?"

"Can I borrow your boat? Please?"

"Sure."

He told me where the key was hidden and the quirks of starting it and offered his cottage as well. I considered that but thought better of it.

An hour later I was on the lake, heading toward Andy's

island. I didn't know exactly what I would do when I got there but wanted to at least take a look.

It felt wonderfully refreshing to be out on the water with the crisp breeze in my face. I pushed the throttle fully forward and flew over the small chop.

Lake Rosseau is a mid-sized lake speckled with hundreds of islands, some little more than granite outcroppings with a few scraggly pines. Andy's island came into view. It was bigger than most, about ten acres. Aside from a narrow walking path, the back half was largely untouched and heavily wooded. I slowed and puttered along the east side, to get a closer look.

As the cottage came into view a police boat pulled out from the nearest dock. The officer waved me away, directing me toward about twenty other boats, all bobbing sixty yards offshore, facing the island. I obediently turned and headed toward them. The officer turned his boat back toward Andy's place.

Several of the boaters had binoculars and were openly trying to see what they could. Others, probably reporters, had cameras with massive zoom lenses and one overcrowded small boat had a camera crew facing a woman who appeared to be taping a report. I pulled down the brim of my cap and motored slowly behind them all, trying to avoid the cameras.

Andy's island had two boathouses and one standalone dock. There were at least a dozen boats tied to the docks, and the island was crawling with police officers and other officials. That was a bit surprising given that the bodies had been discovered four days earlier.

After idling for only seconds, I gently re-engaged my engine and eased away. I slowly motored to the undeveloped side of Andy's island. There was no immediate police presence, so I was able to get closer.

When I was thirty feet from shore, I got a glimpse of the septic field. The field itself was forty or fifty yards long and twenty yards wide. Its entire perimeter was cordoned off with yellow police tape. There was a backhoe resting at the far end and a white-tented area nearby, where the bodies must have been found. Two officers were on the field, mulling around. Another was coming and going from the tent talking to whoever was inside.

Some of the boaters from the cottage side of the island saw how close I was and headed towards me.

Within a few minutes, there were a dozen boats on my side of the island, some closer to shore than me. Several of the boaters were yelling back and forth, discussing the latest news. The fact was, there wasn't much in the way of new information. As is often the case with small town murders, the police were being closed-mouthed about the evidence they had. In this case, with bodies as old as I suspected these to be, they probably knew very little, unless the killer buried their wallets or Bev's purse with them. The corpses' fingerprints would be long gone, so dental records were the most likely means of identifying the victims. I doubted that Bev or Emile's dental records were in any public database, much less a Canadian one.

I felt odd watching the officers. At the very least I was withholding evidence. My every instinct told me I should drive my boat to Andy's dock and ask to talk to the officer in charge and tell him who I thought the bodies were. The problem was, I didn't know what else was in that grave. The only reason the killer buried the bodies on that island was to frame me. If he went to all that trouble, he might have left other incriminating evidence as well. Shit, he might have been watching at that very moment.

I looked around at the other boaters. They seemed to be a mixture of locals and press. No one looked familiar.

I took my engine out of neutral and worked my way through the other boats, heading away from the island. It would be so easy to remain anonymous, to head back to Sandy's cottage and drive home. I started in that direction, accelerating into the wind. I cut behind Andy's island and headed back toward the Windemere Resort, just east of Sandy's cottage.

Everything felt wrong. I'd spent my entire life trying to do the right thing and here I was, involved in the most serious legal issue I'd ever been a part of, and I was doing the wrong thing.

I slowed to almost neutral, barely inching forward. I had children to think about. I had to take care of them and my wife. I couldn't do that from jail.

The tiny waves slapped against my boat. I felt the slight warmth of the early spring sun on my face. I breathed in the scent of the fresh water and the distant pines.

I couldn't just leave. I had to do what was right.

I slowly accelerated and started a wide circle back to Andy's island, to the authorities. It was time to start talking.

As I made the slow turn, I saw another boat coming out from behind the island. There were three men onboard. They seemed to be heading in the general direction of Windemere. I cut a little more to my right, to give them room.

They turned with me. Were they following me? I turned to my left, back toward Windemere and opened the throttle, widening the four-hundred-yard gap between us. They let the gap increase but kept following me.

I'd come all this way to try to figure out who was setting me up. The police could wait.

I continued north, toward Windemere. Testing my pursuers, I gently altered my course, heading northeast. They followed. I made a slow circle to my left, back towards Windemere. Again, they followed. I opened Sandy's poor old engine to full throttle. For thirty seconds the gap between us widened, then it started to narrow. My heart raced. I headed towards the resort, towards what I hoped would be the safety of other people.

Five minutes later, as I approached Windemere's extensive docks, my pursuers were fifty yards behind. I passed a No Wake Zone buoy and slowed my engine. They did too. I was afraid to look back at them but forced myself to. One guy was talking on his cellphone. He was fifty and fat. Neither he nor the driver, a scrawny kid in his early twenties, looked too threatening. But the third guy was massive, maybe 6'4" and at least 250 pounds. I didn't want anything to do with him.

When I was twenty feet from Windemere's dock I turned sharply to my left, in the general direction of Sandy's inlet.

This time, rather than turning with me, they continued straight. I was relieved as they slowed and docked. I headed west, back to Sandy's.

I wasn't sure what to make of the men who'd been following me, but the certainty I'd felt just minutes earlier hadn't diminished. I needed to talk to the police. But I decided to do it on land, in Port Carling. I docked in Sandy's boathouse, carefully secured his boat – double checking each line – and put the key back in its hiding spot.

As I started to leave, a boat entered the inlet – the one that had been following me. There were only two men on board, the driver and the obese guy, who was still on his cell. They must have dropped the third guy off at Windemere.

My car was parked up behind the cottage and I doubted they could see it from the boat. I backed out of the boathouse and hurried to it, hoping I might slip away unnoticed. As I pulled out of Sandy's driveway, I saw an SUV approaching, a silver Chevy Tahoe. Even from inside the truck, the driver looked huge. It was the third guy from the boat, the one they dropped off.

Our cars were getting closer. We had to slow to a crawl to pass on the narrow dirt road. I stared straight at the driver, but he held his hand over the left side of his face, obscuring my view.

If he wanted to follow me, he'd have to turn around in Sandy's driveway. That would buy me a little time. As soon as I passed him I took off, spraying sand and gravel up against the back of his SUV.

Fifty seconds later I reached the main road, spinning onto its pavement. My hotel was to my right, but I turned left and hit the gas. The road meandered so I almost immediately lost sight of Sandy's road in my rearview mirror. At a dangerous seventy miles per hour I passed a half dozen dirt roads on my left, which led to cottages by the lake, and two paved roads on my right. I turned right onto the next paved road and headed north. There was no way he could know which road I'd taken.

I felt sure I lost him, but kept speeding nonetheless. If I kept driving, I'd be in Toronto in less than two hours and across the border soon after that. But I had to go back to my hotel. My luggage was still there.

All I knew about the driver was that he was big, dark-haired and drove a silver Chevy Tahoe. He and his colleagues in the boat were my only leads. If they were following me, they knew who I was and must have been waiting for me at Andy's. And if they were looking for me at Andy's, they were either the killers or working for the killers.

They were my only clue. I had to find out who they were.

Reluctantly I turned around and headed back toward Windemere, where they'd dropped the guy in the Tahoe.

Ten nerve-racking minutes later I made a right onto the road that led to the Windemere Resort Hotel complex, the surrounding buildings and the lake. I kept checking my rearview mirror. If the Tahoe came up behind me, I'd be trapped. But there was no one there.

As the road wound down toward the lake, I got caught behind an old guy in a hat driving fifteen miles per hour. Two cars caught up with us, but neither was the silver SUV. The lake came into view. The old man took the main road, straight down the hill to the hotel and the water. I turned right onto a side road and parked in a lot behind a building there, just up the hill from the hotel. If the guy in the Tahoe was ahead of me or stayed on the main access road to meet his partners at the lake, he wouldn't see my car.

I took off my navy fleece and put on a baseball cap. It was a little chilly wearing only a dark-green golf shirt, but I had to change my appearance. The main access road was to the left of the hotel. On foot, I took a sleepy-looking alternate road on the right. For most of my descent I was hidden from the main road by the hotel.

Once I passed the hotel, ten-foot decorative pines lined each side of my street, so I doubted anyone could see me from the dock. When I was a hundred yards from the water, I stopped behind a tree and pretended to answer an email on my phone. Several pedestrians passed but none took a second glance my way.

The boat that followed me to Sandy's was back at the dock with two men standing beside it. I realized it was a boat taxi and that the young driver was probably just a local they'd hired. The other man, the obese black-haired guy, was still on his phone. It looked as though I'd beaten the Tahoe back. While I could see the dock and the boat, I couldn't see much of the main access road or the hotel's parking lot. To get a better view I had to get to the hotel which was across two hundred feet of manicured lawn, all plainly visible from the dock.

I couldn't risk being spotted so I hurried back up the same alternate road, under the cover of the pines. I entered the back of the hotel, then made my way to the extensive lobby with its big windows and panoramic views of the lake and the access road. So long as the car's driver wasn't in the lobby and the two men I was aware of didn't have anyone else working with them, I could safely watch.

The guy by the boat was still on the phone.

Twenty minutes later I saw a silver Tahoe SUV coming down the access road. I hurried toward the back windows of the hotel to watch him. He parked, got out of the car and walked along the access road down to the dock. He was a big, tough-looking guy. Standing well back from the window so he couldn't see me, I took a picture of him with my phone. Once he was well past, I hurried through the lobby to the back exit and parking lot. I grabbed a softball-sized rock from the side of the lot and hurried to the Tahoe. I was shocked to see that it had New York plates.

I checked the passenger side door. It was locked. I took the rock and was about to smash it into the passenger side front window but stopped. I grabbed a pebble and crouched. Largely hidden by the car, I let the air out of the front right tire. It seemed to take forever. I could feel sweat beading on my forehead.

After three interminable minutes, it was flat.

I peeked over the hood, scanning the lot and the access road. I didn't see anyone. I picked up the big rock and wrapped my baseball cap around it, then smashed the passenger window as hard as I could. It made a hell of a noise, but nothing happened. I hit it a few more times. Still nothing. I glared at the rock, like it was its fault.

Ignoring the noise, I kept hammering. Astonishingly, no one came running out of the hotel to see what all the racket was about. "Just fucking break," I panted. After what seemed like another eternity, the window cracked, then broke away.

I unlocked the door and opened it. I checked the glove

compartment and found registration papers and an insurance card. I took them. As I rifled through the center console, two men came out from behind the hotel, walking toward me – my men.

I backed out of the passenger side of the car, with my face below the dashboard, out of their line of sight. When I was just about out of the car I noticed a black backpack behind the driver's seat. The men were getting closer. I could hear their shoes on the gravel. I sort of lunged back in and grabbed the backpack. I slid out and crept backward staying low. I reached the next car, four spots away, then stood, facing away from the two men. I walked purposely in the opposite direction toward my own car, which was still a quarter of a mile away, in the next lot up across another street.

I didn't look back but could hear the two men talking. As they approached their car, I heard one say, "What the fuck? We've got a flat."

I didn't look back. I just kept walking, a little faster now.

A second voice, "Shit. Someone broke into our car. They broke my window."

I walked even faster. I was a hundred and fifty yards from them, but still in the open parking lot and a long way from my car.

I wanted to run but kept walking fast.

"Fuck."

I could picture them looking around, spotting me.

"Hey, you!"

They must have seen me. I glanced over my shoulder.

"It's him."

As soon as I heard that, I took off in a sprint for my car. I was a couple hundred yards ahead of them and, I hoped, a lot faster. I was afraid they might start shooting at me and, ridiculously, wondered if I should serpentine. My mind raced.

The shortest distance between two points is a straight line. I ran straight.

I reached the road and then the lawn surrounding the building in front of my lot. I looked over my shoulder again. They were still chasing, but slowly. I ran around the building to my car. I tossed their backpack onto the passenger seat and hit the start button. I put it into drive and peeled out, toward the exit. I saw one of the two men in my rearview mirror. The big guy from the Tahoe.

The parking lot funneled into a driveway that led out to the road I had just crossed. The second man, the fat guy from the dock, was doing his best to sprint to block my exit. He was going to get there before I did. I cut sharply to my left, away from him and over a nice lawn.

The fat guy extended his arms. He was holding a gun. He pointed it at me.

I sped across the lawn toward the road. There was a car approaching us. The fat guy whipped his hands behind his back, hiding the gun from the people in the car. I bounced over the curb onto the road just as they passed, swerving left to avoid them.

I accelerated to the main access road and out of Windemere. God. My heart was racing. I was going sixty in a thirty zone. Mustering what self-discipline I could, I slowed to forty-five.

I calmed myself and tried to figure out what to do.

I thought about just heading west, but I needed to get back to my motel room to get my stuff. It would take them a while to get their tire fixed, even though it only needed to be reinflated. At least they didn't know where I was going or where I was staying.

Twenty minutes later I was there. I quickly gathered my things and tossed them in the trunk of the car. Then I walked to the office to give them my room key. The woman who ran the place was sitting behind the reception desk.

"Hi. I'm going to checkout a day early."

"Is something wrong?"

"No. It's just that my plans have changed." Boy, was that true.

"Okay. Let me just go into the back room and get some cash for your refund."

I swear I could hear a clock behind her ticking. "That's alright. I feel bad for cancelling on you. You can just keep it."

Her face brightened. "Thanks. Have a safe trip."

I turned to leave.

"Oh, did your friends find you?"

"My friends?"

"The two American guys. They came by last night ten minutes after you left for the diner I told you about, asking for you."

"Asking for me? Did they mention my name?" I'd registered under a fake name.

"I think so. They knew your room number."

"What did you tell them?"

She looked concerned. "I'm sorry. I told them they just missed you. I hope I didn't do anything wrong."

I tried to sound convincing. "Oh no. It's nothing. I thought I was supposed to meet them for breakfast this morning. We got our signals crossed."

She smiled, not buying my lie.

I got back in my car and headed south, again trying not to speed.

If they were at my hotel last night it meant they hadn't spotted me at Tim's. I hadn't gone there until this morning. They must have been following me before then. The Tahoe had New York plates. Christ. They'd followed me all the way from Connecticut.

My heart started to race.

What if they'd placed a tracking device on my car?

But if they had, the Tahoe guy would have followed me straight from Sandy's. He hadn't. He got to Windemere Hotel forty minutes after I did, and it was pretty clear that when I was watching them there, they had no idea I was around. Nonetheless, I pulled over at the next gas station and thoroughly inspected my car for a device. I found nothing.

I opened the backpack. The outer pocket had a wallet and an American passport. I opened the passport to look at the picture. It was of the guy driving the car. His name was Gerald Farro and he was born in Maryland in 1975. I opened the wallet. It had his driver's license and a ton of cash. I checked his address: Mount Vernon, New York, a suburb not too far from the city or Greenwich. I fished through the rest of the pack. There was a fleece, a rain jacket and, at the bottom, a pistol and two ammunition clips.

I was in so far over my head.

The fat guy had a gun too. How could they possibly have gotten guns across the border?

Maybe they didn't. Not if they were working for Hendrie. He had drivers coming to and from Canada all the time. The guy was a mob boss. He could have easily had some of his Canadian contacts meet Farro and the other guy and give them guns and ammunition.

Chapter 22:

I called Jenny and told her everything. My overriding concern was for her and the boys. If the killer was after me, he might go after them as well.

She wanted me to go to the police. I said that I wanted to as well, but that I couldn't. Not yet. Aside from the threat to our safety, if there was even a hint that I was tied to murder or blackmail, every client I had would pull their funds and I'd go out of business. I had to try to clear my name.

After a lot of discussion, I convinced her that she and the boys should go into hiding. A friend of ours, a very wealthy friend named Brenda Burton, had a couple of houses in Telluride, Colorado. Without going into detail, we told her that we were afraid for our safety and asked if Jenny and the boys could stay at one of the houses anonymously. She'd said of course.

Next we had to convince the boys. For the time being we thought the oldest one, who lived in London, was safe. It took some serious convincing, but we talked the two who lived in New York and the one in Phoenix to tell their employers that they had a family emergency and simply had to leave. The boys resisted, but when Jenny told them she legitimately feared for their lives, they acquiesced.

Our Phoenix-based son took buses from Phoenix to Durango and on to Telluride. He paid cash for his tickets and everything he purchased along the way.

Jenny took $8,000 in cash out of our checking account. She and the boys took various trains to Ronkonkoma on Long Island and then paid cash for cabs to MacArthur Airport.

My older brother had a house in Nantucket and through him, I knew a pilot who made money on the side by doing cash charters from Connecticut to Nantucket in the summertime.

I called him and asked if he was willing to fly my wife and two of my sons to Lincoln, Nebraska. His plane, a single-engine Cessna Skyhawk seated six and had a range of seven hundred miles. He said he would make the trip, but that he would probably have to stop a few times along the way.

We agreed on a price and six hours later he met Jenny and the boys at MacArthur.

He flew them uneventfully to a municipal airport forty-five minutes outside of Lincoln. Jenny's brother, Thomas, met them there. He lent Jenny his Suburban and she and the boys headed west.

Chapter 23:

Once Jenny and the boys were safe, I was free to think, to focus on figuring out who the two guys who followed me were.

I decided to get rid of my brother-in-law Chris' car so it wouldn't be so easy for them to follow me again. I called Chris and asked him to rent a car and drop it off at the train station in Mamaroneck, New York and to pay to park it there for three days. I implored him to do it immediately, so that Farro's partners or employer didn't have time to have people following him.

Then I got rid of Farro's gun. I took it apart and threw the pieces and the ammunition clips into a lake, an hour west of Ottawa. When I stopped for food, I got rid of most of the rest of his stuff. I kept his wallet, passport and car registration.

I took my time driving home, stopping and sleeping for a few hours at a rest stop along New York State Thruway. The next morning, I swapped my brother-in-law's car for the rental at the train station and checked into a cheap, cash motel in southern Westchester County, halfway between my house and the city.

I did a background check and discovered Farro had a criminal record and had been convicted of burglary and assault. He spent four years in a New York State penitentiary.

The fact that Farro and his partner found my motel in Muskoka really bothered me. If they had simply been waiting at the island to see if I showed up, it would have meant they knew about the island in advance and had to be the killers. But they visited the motel *before* I went to Andy's island which meant they had to have followed me all the way from Connecticut. That complicated things. It meant they weren't necessarily tied to Emile and Bev's killer.

Except they did find me at the island, on the boat. If they

didn't know about Bev and Emile's bodies, how could they have done that?

I thought about it for a while. Before I called Sandy to ask if I could use his boat, I drove to his cottage. When I got there, I'd gone down to his boathouse to see if he still had a boat there. He did. I sat on his dock for an hour to run my models so that I could call in my trades after I called Sandy from the payphone at Windemere. If they were watching me from their car, Farro could have driven back to Windemere and dropped off the fat guy to rent the boat taxi. While I was doing my fund work Farro could have driven back to Sandy's while the fat guy in the boat taxi could have approached and hung around on the lake off Sandy's cove. When I left in Sandy's boat, Farro could have driven back to Windemere, and the fat guy and the boat taxi driver could have picked him up there. The lake around Sandy's and Windemere is wide open, so they could have picked him up without losing sight of my boat.

I knew I was reaching for an explanation, but it was at least plausible. And it left open the possibility that Hendrie and his men weren't associated with the killer and, until I led them to the island, hadn't been aware of the bodies there. Any of the five people who knew I knew of their blackmailing could have hired thugs to follow me to find Coulon.

Or to kill me.

103

Chapter 24:

The next morning, I got up at 5:30 and drove from my motel to the Mount Vernon address on Farro's driver's license. His neighborhood was nice: two-storey, four-bedroom houses, a lot of Tudors on quarter-acre well-maintained lots. I turned on to his street. His silver Tahoe was parked in the driveway of the second house on the right, next to a grey minivan. There was a clear garbage bag taped over the front passenger side window.

It was 6:15 and the house was dark. I went to a coffee shop and picked up some breakfast. Thirty minutes later I drove by again. Some lights were on.

The blocks in his part of Mount Vernon were small and there was on-street parking. I drove around the block and parked just around the corner from Farro's house, with a clear view of his driveway. At 7:40 a woman who must have been Farro's wife left the house with two kids. It looked like she was driving them to school.

Farro wasn't far behind. This was the first time I could really look him over. He was truly massive. He looked like an NFL linebacker. Gerald was not someone I wanted to mess with. He hopped into his Tahoe and headed out. I followed from as far back as I dared. He led me to the Cross County and then the Hutchison River Parkway. We were heading in the direction of Greenwich.

There was a lot of rush hour traffic so it was slow going, but it was easy for me to hide six to eight cars back. He exited onto 287 and then again into Port Chester. Five minutes later he pulled into Hendrie Trucking.

I kept going. I knew everything I needed to know about Farro. Hendrie had Farro and the other guy follow me all the way to Canada.

I headed back to my motel and considered what to do. Within minutes, I had a plan.

I walked to a Walgreens down the street from the motel and bought a medium-sized manila envelope and some paper. I put Farro's passport, car registration and wallet with all its contents, including $1720 in cash, into the envelope with a note instructing him to have Hendrie call me. I gave him the number of one of my two burner phones. I drove back to Farro's house and put the envelope into his mailbox.

His wife apparently saw me pull up to the curbside mailbox and stepped out the front door. She was an attractive blonde.

"Can I help you?"

"No thanks. I just have something for your husband. I didn't mean to bother you with it."

I pointed to the mailbox, smiled, got back in my car and drove away. I could see her walking to the mailbox in my rearview mirror.

Twenty minutes later my phone buzzed.

"Hello."

"Osgood?"

"I don't want to talk to you. Have Hendrie call me."

An hour later it buzzed again.

"Hello."

"We should talk."

This time it was Hendrie.

"Okay. Where?"

"Come to my office."

"No."

"Where then?"

"I'll be sitting on one of the benches across the street from the Greenwich police station. Let's meet there."

He hesitated then said, "When?"

"I'm here now."

'I'll be there in a half an hour."

Twenty minutes later Farro and the fat guy from the boat walked up to my bench. Farro spoke first.

"Mr. Hendrie is in that black Mercedes." He pointed to a car illegally parked about a half a block from the police station. It was idling. "Go meet him there."

He was visibly pissed.

"What are you mad about? I gave you your wallet back."

"Fuck you. Let's go."

As a police officer stepped out the front door of the police station, I smiled. "No. This is good."

Farro glared at me, but looked toward Hendrie's car and shook his head.

The front passenger-side door opened and Hendrie stepped out.

The passing cop said, "Sir, you can't park there."

Hendrie didn't respond. He ignored the cop and walked toward me.

Farro's partner from the boat, the fat guy, saw Hendrie give him a look and started to sort of jog to him and the cop. It was comical.

He passed Hendrie about halfway between me and his car. Hendrie said something to him, and the breathless fat guy continued his slowing jog, toward the increasingly angry cop.

I stood as Hendrie approached the bench. Farro loomed over me.

Hendrie looked at me and then at the police station. "Let's go for a walk."

He saw me start to object and pointed toward Greenwich Avenue, which is an east coast, lesser version of Rodeo Drive. The avenue was busy with pedestrian shoppers and, reassuringly, ridiculous traffic cops in white gloves on every corner, wasting taxpayer dollars and needlessly slowing the flow of pedestrians and cars every fifty to one hundred yards.

I nodded and started toward the avenue, beside Hendrie. Farro followed, just behind.

Hendrie spoke first. "Who's buried on that island?"

What a loaded question. If he killed them, he knew. If he didn't, he was pretty sure. Either way, there was no point in me stating the obvious.

"So, it is Coulon and his girl."

It was a statement, not a question. But the way he said it implied I was confirming what he suspected. Or he was playing me.

I remained silent.

As we walked, he thought for a minute.

"Why did you go up there? What did you hope to accomplish?"

I considered my answer and didn't see any downside in being honest. "I wanted to find out what happened to them. To find any lead I could." I paused. "And I found you."

Hendrie corrected me. "We found you."

I was in an incredibly precarious position. Hendrie probably suspected that I knew he laundered money through Royal Foods. Emile must have tried to blackmail him or Walker for money laundering and Hendrie may have had him killed in response.

I tried to hide my fear and asked, "Why? Why have your guys follow me?"

I thought I knew the answer, but I wanted to hear it from him. This time, he indulged me.

"To see if you'd lead us to Coulon." He smiled. "And you did."

"But how did you know I was going to Canada? You can't have been following me all this time? It's been almost six years since they disappeared."

Hendrie kept walking but slowed. "We got a call. Someone left us a message telling us that you were on Coulon's trail."

"Who?"

"I don't know."

"But you believed it? You had me followed all the way to Canada because of one anonymous call?"

"It worked."

I was beginning to get really pissed off at myself. Hendrie and whoever had called him were constantly two steps ahead of me. I really needed to up my game.

We walked quietly for about a minute. Two over-coiffed, shopping-bag-toting trophy wives passed us. We shared a thought and continued up the sidewalk.

I broke the silence.

"What happens now?"

Hendrie shrugged. He didn't want to threaten me. If he did all I had to do was walk up to one of the traffic cops and start talking. But even if I was safe now, how could I know my family and I would remain safe?

I looked him straight in the eye. "Do you know what the statute of limitations is on money laundering?"

That got his attention, but he didn't respond.

"It's five years."

Again, he didn't respond.

"When Emile and I researched Royal Foods, we were looking at financial data pertaining to 2008 and 2009."

He didn't say anything.

I continued, "I think it's a reasonable assumption that once Emile started, um, talking to you or to Mr. Walker, that any 'activities' you had with RFC stopped. That was more than eight years ago."

He was a very smart man. He hadn't said a single word that could get him into trouble. Even if I was recording our conversation, which I wasn't, he hadn't compromised himself in the least.

He stopped walking and turned to face me.

"I haven't got anything on you, Mr. Hendrie."

He seemed to ponder that and started to walk again, still up the avenue, away from his car.

"Unless you were involved in what happened in Muskoka on that island, you have nothing to worry about as far as I am concerned. I've got nothing on you. And I'm comfortable that you weren't involved in that. If you were, I wouldn't be here now."

Hendrie didn't acknowledge my point, but he got my message.

To further my point I added, "I honestly don't think you would even know about the island if I hadn't led Gerald and his buddy right to it." I looked over my shoulder to Farro. He wasn't amused by my use of his first name.

This time Hendrie looked right at me. "How do you know about that island? How do you know it's them?"

"A friend of mine owns it."

He considered that for a moment, then burst out laughing.

"They're fucking framing you. Christ, Osgood, you can't get out of your own way."

He was laughing so hard that other people on the sidewalk were turning to look at us.

He stopped and turned to face me. Still grinning broadly, he said, "It was a nice touch giving Gerald his wallet back, with every penny of his money."

I looked at Farro. He still wasn't amused.

Hendrie looked me in the eye and extended his hand. "Alright. We're good."

"Yeah?"

He nodded again to reassure me. "Yeah."

Chapter 25:

It was a huge relief to check Hendrie off my list. While I thought the other people Emile blackmailed might come after me, Hendrie was the only one I thought might come after my family.

Jenny and I discussed the situation and agreed that it was probably safe for her and the boys to come home. I checked out of my crappy motel and went home too.

But I was still in trouble. At some point the police in Ontario would identify the bodies and once they did, I would become a suspect, probably the prime suspect, in the murders. But unless the killer left some clues behind, that might take a while. I was partially relieved that after five days, the Canadian police hadn't contacted me. While I didn't think my DNA was in any national database, my fingerprints were. Like every employee of every bank in the country, I was fingerprinted the day I started my first job after college, at City Federal Bank, when I was twenty-two. If the killers had left anything with my prints with the bodies, I'd have already been in custody.

But the real killer was still out there, watching me. He had to be the one who told Hendrie to follow me, maybe to try to frame him too. He was the only one who could have known I'd go north once I heard the bodies were discovered.

Over the next twenty-four hours I tried to figure out what to do. For safety's sake, I decided to write a letter to the local authorities, to Mike Eastmure of the Greenwich police, in case anything happened to me. In the letter I outlined everything I knew about the murders and Emile's blackmail scheme, including the names of the people I felt he'd blackmailed. I left the letter in my desk at home, with Mike Eastmure's name on the sealed envelope.

Early the next morning, two days after I'd driven home, I headed back to Canada, back to Muskoka.

This time I took the most direct route. I got to Toronto at dusk and spent the night there. After a fitful night's sleep, I checked out at 7am and headed north. I didn't notice anyone following me, but having missed Farro and his partner all the way from Connecticut to Ontario on my last trip, I wasn't re-assured.

At 9am, as I was approaching the lake area, I considered asking my friend Sandy if I could borrow his boat again but decided against it. There was no need to drag him into my mess. I found a boat taxi.

The driver was an engaging man in his late sixties.

"Where to?"

"Just head out the river onto Lake Rosseau. I'll direct you from there."

"You're the boss."

Ten minutes later we were out of the river.

"Head toward Windemere, please."

Andy's island was the second island from the mouth of the river. Once we were past the first island, Andy's new cottage came into view. It was early enough that there weren't any gawkers, but there were several boats tied to the docks and a few police officers walking around.

"Did you hear about what happened up here?"

"I did. Anything new on who they are?"

"Not really. Two bodies, a man and woman. That's all I've heard."

"Is there a suspect?"

"The island's owner."

"Really?"

"Not the current owner. He's the one who had the septic tank dug up. Not even the police think he'd be stupid enough to do that if he'd buried bodies there."

"Then who?"

"His uncle, the guy he bought it from."

I couldn't believe it. Tim was the suspect. Wow, did they ever get that one wrong.

The driver went on. "The uncle, Tim Allen, died a couple of years ago, but I guess the bodies have been there since before then."

I let him drive a little past Andy's house, toward Windemere. My heart was racing. Tim had been my friend and had been incredibly good to me over the years. Everyone would think bad things about him and his family. Because of me. My face burned with shame.

Enough. I had to end it and end it now.

"Turn back and head to the main dock. Where the officers are."

The old guy looked up at me. "I don't think they'll allow us anywhere near the island."

"Just try."

As we turned toward the dock a uniformed Ontario Provincial Police officer heard the sound of the engine and waved us off. The driver started to obey him, to turn away.

"Keep going."

"Look mister, I'm not going to disobey the police."

"Just do it. I'll take responsibility."

Reluctantly, he turned back to the dock. The officer became more agitated and again waved us off. I waved back and held up a single finger. The officer looked skeptical, but waved us in.

As we got within earshot the driver shifted the boat into neutral.

"You can't dock here. Turn back and head off."

The driver looked from the officer to me.

"I need to talk to whoever is in charge here. I'm coming ashore."

The policeman considered sending us off again but decided to give me a listen. As the driver pulled up beside the dock, the officer put a foot on the portside gunwale.

"What's your business here?"

I stepped from the boat onto the dock.

"I know who's buried up there, whose bodies you found."

That got his attention. He looked from me to the boat taxi driver. The driver's jaw was dropped.

"Who's in charge?"

The officer kept his foot on the gunwale, but stood up straight, apparently trying to decide if I looked credible. I was wearing khakis, a dress shirt, brown bucks and a navy zip-up fleece. I was clean shaven and had closely cropped, gray hair. I looked mature, but not so old that I might be looney.

"Okay. Come on."

The taxi driver, who thought he was in on the biggest piece of news he'd ever come across, started to get out of the boat. The officer held up a hand.

"Wait here. I doubt we'll be long."

Glad to be allowed to stay, he jumped up onto the dock and tied on.

The officer led me off the dock, up the slate steps to the cottage.

"What's your name?"

"Phil Osgood."

"You American?"

"Yes. From Connecticut."

"What makes you think you know who the bodies are?"

"Look Officer, just take me to your boss. You won't regret it."

He gave me another look but continued up the steps.

As we reached the patio off Andy's living room, another officer approached us.

"Where's Inspector Houston?"

The constable said, "He's up by the tent. What's going on?"

"This guy says he knows who was buried here."

That got his attention too. He followed us around the cottage to the septic field. With this closer view I could see a tent covering the spot where the bodies must have been found. It was on the back portion of the field about as far from the cottage as could be. There were holes all over the field. They must have been looking for more bodies. Two plain-clothed officers were standing beside the tent.

One of them, a tall, lean, weary looking man in his early fifties stepped toward us. He was wearing a gray suit with a navy-blue tie. He appeared to be in charge.

"What's up, Bill? Who's this?"

"This is Mr. Osgood. He says he has information about the bodies."

Again, that got everyone's attention. I watched as the detective looked me over.

He stepped toward me. "I'm Inspector Jim Houston. Who are you, sir?"

I stepped forward and extended my hand, more out of habit than anything else.

"I'm Philip Osgood. I'm from the United States, from Connecticut." I paused. "I'm pretty sure I know who you found in that grave."

The inspector looked me over again, shook my hand and seemed to make a decision. "Okay, Mr. Osgood. Follow me."

He led me into Andy's cottage. The others tried to follow. Houston waved them off, but nodded to the constable who met me on the dock. The three of us walked into the mostly finished cottage and Houston led us to the dining room. He motioned toward one of the side seats at a large folding table and took one on the opposite side, directly across from me. The constable sat beside him.

"Okay, Mr. Osgood. Whose bodies do you think we found?"

I could hear the skepticism in his voice and gathered myself. "I think you have the bodies of a man named Emile Coulon and a woman named Beverly Sutton. Emile is 5'7" or 5'8" and was seventy-one when he died. Bev was maybe 5'10" and sixty years old, though I'm less sure of her age."

Nothing I had read about the bodies had said anything other than that they were a man and a woman.

Houston looked straight at me, directly into my eyes. I looked back. "Hang on a second." He stood and walked back outside. He returned with another detective in plain clothes. He nodded toward her. "This is Inspector Milne." She nodded and set up a recording device in front of me.

Houston watched until Milne was almost done and then rhetorically asked, "Do you mind if we record our conversation?"

I nodded, then for the benefit of the recording added, "No problem."

Houston looked to Milne, who established the date and time, then asked me for my full name, date of birth and address. Once that was done Houston took over again.

"So tell us, Mr. Osgood, what makes you think you know who we found buried here?"

I had spent a great deal of time considering how I would answer that question and, still unsure I led with, "Because I think whoever killed them is trying to frame me for their murders."

For the next two hours I explained my relationship with Coulon, the blackmail scheme and how I knew the Allen's, whose cottage we were sitting in.

Once the officers were convinced I was somewhat credible, we drove down to the provincial police's regional headquarters in Orillia and repeated the process.

After over five hours of questioning, Houston started to move beyond the facts as I knew them.

"Why do you think someone would go to the trouble of bringing these people all the way up to Canada to kill them or hide the bodies?"

"I think there are a few possible reasons."

I paused, but Houston, who'd already shown himself to be a patient man, simply waited.

"First, Emile and Bev may have come here on their own."

"Why?"

"Back in 2012 they left a false trail to Florida. They might have made enough from their years of blackmailing that they decided to just move away and live off their stolen money. Or maybe one of the people they blackmailed was after them and they were hiding. Either way, they could have come to Canada and stopped at Tim's."

"Why would they?

"I'd shown them pictures over the years and they both loved boats. Maybe they figured in late October it would be a safe place to hide for a few days."

Houston didn't seem to buy that idea, and I wasn't sure I did either.

"But if, as you say, the killer did bring or lure them here, all the way to Canada, maybe he did it because there was a very good chance the bodies would never be found, at least not in the killer's lifetime. And even if they were found, and if the police could somehow determine the victims' identities, they'd eventually be tied to me."

Houston thought about that for a minute then asked, "Then why do you think they didn't leave evidence linking you to the bodies in the grave?"

"I have to admit, I've been afraid they might have. I suppose they didn't because if I hadn't come forward, there was a good chance you would never have discovered Emile and Bev's identities. I suspect that the killer or killers hoped to get away with the murders more than anything else. And they figured that if they left clues tying me to the bodies, they might be opening a can of worms that might otherwise never have been opened. But if you did somehow identify the bodies, they could pin it on me."

Houston and his colleagues pondered that for a while.

Contemplating what they might be thinking I added, "If you think about it, I had a motive: they made me an unwitting party to a decade-long blackmail scheme. I had opportunity: Tim gave me access to the cottage during the time when they may have been killed or at least buried here. I was here. And finally, I don't have an alibi."

Chapter 26:

I spent the next three days being questioned in Orillia. I wasn't under arrest, but I was under constant surveillance.

On the fourth day we moved to Toronto. By that time the Canadian authorities had been able to get dental records from the American authorities and confirmed that the bodies were Emile and Bev.

When news of the identities broke, Canadian and American news teams swarmed Muskoka, Toronto and Greenwich.

With the strong extradition treaties between the US and Canada and the lack of any concrete evidence implicating me, Houston and his superiors allowed me to return to the States. I retold my story to the Greenwich Police, the Connecticut State Police and the FBI.

In an effort to identify other possible suspects in the murders, Canadian and American authorities questioned me extensively about the blackmail victims I'd identified. With some, like Patel, the Medicare fraud doctor, and Graber, the embezzling banker, I simply told them everything I knew. If either of those two was arrested, I simply didn't care. But with the others, I was more circumspect. In Hendrie's case, I told them I suspected Coulon had tried to blackmail Hendrie and Walker for money laundering, but that we'd never been able to prove it. I admitted that I had met with Hendrie and been able to convince him that I had nothing on him. With Senator Rawlings, I admitted that we had caught him in an extramarital affair, but didn't mention that it was with a man.

Eventually the media got a hold of Coulon's blackmail scheme and my role in it. At best, I was portrayed as a dumbass, wanna-be detective – not a wholly inaccurate assessment. At worst, as a murderer. The institutional investors I had in my fund withdrew their investments, and my assets and revenues were cut by 80%. By most people's standards I was still making a good living, but anytime anyone reduces their income by 80%, they and their families feel it.

My normal life was gone. So was Jenny's. The media hounded us for weeks. We could barely go out. Even after their interest waned, things were different. Some friends abandoned us. Others tried to glom onto us, wanting to be part of something so newsworthy. A few remained true.

It was brutal. Before I knew I'd been party to Coulon's blackmail I'd rarely thought I was the smartest guy in the room, but I never thought I was the dumbest. Emile had proved me wrong.

I wanted to go to my office every day, to manage my fund and hide, but at first, I couldn't. I was still renting space from my friend Paul, and I didn't want to taint his reputation by being associated with me. Before he had to ask, I called him and told him I was moving offices. I found a dingy spot on the wrong side of Greenwich. It was a bleak place that suited my mood.

I went there every day early and worked and exercised, running forty to fifty miles a week. That helped, but only a little.

One day about six months later my phone rang. It wasn't ringing much at the time and it startled me.

"Phil, this is Howard Rawlings. I'm out front in a black suburban. Come out here."

He ended the call without waiting for a response. I looked out my office window and saw his car. I remembered leaving a note about my location the last time I met him. This time I wasn't worried.

As I exited my building the newly-elected junior senator from Connecticut powered down his window and nodded. Once again, I walked around to the passenger side and hopped in. As soon as I closed the door he pulled out.

"How are you doing?"

I looked over at him, unsure of what he wanted. He looked ahead, keeping his eye on the road.

"Fine, I guess. Congratulations on your election."

"Thanks."

He didn't say anything for a moment. We drove along Railroad Avenue, heading east past the train station. I chuckled to myself as he turned right at the bottom of Greenwich Avenue, under the tracks. He was back on the same route we took the last time.

"Am I going to have to walk home again? It looks like it's going to rain."

Rawlings laughed. "I appreciate the way you handled all of this with the police."

He looked from the road to me.

I simply nodded.

"You didn't have to do what you did."

"I told you before, I have no interest in hurting you or Mrs. Rawlings. I'm sorry I had to mention you at all, to tell them that you'd been blackmailed for having an extramarital affair, but I was – and am – fighting to prove my innocence in all of this."

Rawlings shrugged and smiled. "You didn't hurt me at all, Phil. You could have, but you didn't."

I shrugged.

He looked at me again and said, "Thank you."

This time he drove me back to my office.

A month later my office phone rang again. An investor from a fund of funds I'd never heard of said he had been reviewing my numbers and that he was interested in making an investment. We spoke on and off for a few weeks and met several times. A month later he called and said he'd like to invest $100 million in my fund.

I did the mandated post 9/11 checks on the source of the funds and everything was fine. Ten weeks after my meeting with Rawlings, my fund was twice the size it had been before the withdrawals.

Chapter 27:

While the new investment took care of my financial issues, my reputation was still ruined. I was, to the best of my knowledge, the only suspect in a double homicide. The police didn't have enough on me to press charges, but they weren't in any hurry to declare my innocence. But my reputation wasn't what I fixated on, not by a long shot. Someone had killed two people and was getting away with it.

At the best of times, I have the sort of personality that doesn't let me leave problems alone. If something doesn't strike me as quite right, I poke at it, shove it this way and that, overturn it and then overturn it again. I obsess.

This was the worst of times. The murders consumed me. I discussed them to the point that Jenny sat me down and shared some feelings she was having about the pleasure of living with me. Even with that, I didn't change. I couldn't. I did however learn to keep my thoughts to myself.

I wasn't kind enough to forgive Emile for using me but didn't think he deserved to die for it. Bev's murder was worse. It gnawed at me. I supposed that Emile might have convinced her to go along with blackmailing people, especially if she discovered it after the fact, like I did. But I really had trouble believing she'd allow Emile to use me the way he had. I wanted to find the killer as much for her sake as mine.

With the trail in Connecticut and Ontario cold, I flew to Chicago.

The morning I arrived, I went to the office Emile had used in Winnetka, an affluent suburb north of the city. The current occupant of his old office was a college prep franchise. They'd only been there for a few months and didn't know anything about Emile. But they did tell me where I could find their landlord. He was just down the street.

I walked the three blocks and entered his two-story building, a house converted into office space, and knocked on his office door. When I did, I heard the sound of a dog getting up behind the door. The dog didn't bark, but I could hear the unmistakable jingle of his collar and tags. A deep voice behind the door said, "Come in."

I opened the door and was immediately greeted by the dog. He was an incredibly happy black and white furry-looking guy with a patch over one eye. As I reached to pet him, he jumped up, resting his two front paws on my hips. His cheery face made me laugh, as did the amused voice of his owner who said, "Stanley, get down!"

With Stanley still up, happy to be petted, his owner shook his head and stood. "I'm sorry. Ever since he lost his eye, I've been letting him get away with murder and he knows it."

I kept petting him and laughed. "It's fine. He's a good old boy."

The man, an affable fellow about my age, came from around his desk and extended his right hand as he gently pulled Stanley down with his left. "I'm Jeff Greisch. What can I do for you?"

I shook his hand and said, "Hi, Mr. Greisch. I'm Phil Osgood."

"It's Jeff. Nice to meet you, Phil. What brings you here?"

He motioned to one of the seats in front of his desk and sat back down behind it. Stanley plopped down by me, a new person to pet him.

"I'm here to inquire about a former tenant of yours, a man named Emile Coulon."

At the mention of Emile's name, Greisch's demeanor changed. He was still friendly, but he seemed more alert, a little on guard.

With unmasked scorn, he said, "Coulon. Yeah. He was a piece of work."

I nodded. "That he was." After few seconds of us nodding in agreement I said, "I understand he rented office space from you, over on Main Street."

Greisch looked me right in the eye and said, "He did. He fooled me. Not many people do, but he did."

I waited for him to expand on that, but he didn't. Instead he said, "But not as badly as he fooled you."

My brilliant reputation had apparently reached Illinois. Perfect.

"You're right about that." I didn't have to pretend to look abashed. "How'd he fool you?"

"He stiffed me out of a few months of rent."

"When was that, if you don't mind me asking?"

Greisch reached forward and woke up his desktop computer. He clicked a few keys on the keyboard and pulled up Coulon's account. "Last time I saw him was in August of 2012. And that's the last time he paid his rent. I left the place alone for a few more months, then I cleaned it out."

"Did you ever hear from him again?"

"No. Not a word. Next time I heard about him was when you identified his body up in Ontario."

"You heard about that?"

"Are you kidding? Everyone in Winnetka was all over that story. You of all people know what it's like when murder touches small towns like ours. We all read every piece of news we can."

"Yeah, I do know what you mean. Did the police ever question you?"

"Perfunctorily. When I heard he and his girlfriend were dead, I contacted the Winnetka PD and told 'em Coulon had rented office space from me. It was clear they already knew he'd been in town. They came in a few times, asked a few questions and looked through his files. But so far as I know, nothing ever came of it."

"He left his files? Here? What happened to them?"

"I still have some of them. They're in the basement of his building. Given how much rent he owed me the police said I could do what I wanted with the stuff he left behind, the stuff they didn't take. But most of it was mine anyway – furniture he was renting with the office. They took some of his files and asked me to keep the rest for a while."

"Do you think I could look at them?"

He considered it for a bit and said, "What the hell. Wanna go over now?" Without even waiting for me to answer he stood up and said, "Come on, Stanley."

The three of us made our way from his office toward Emile's old place. Stanley walked happily beside Greisch without a leash.

"If you don't mind my asking, why are you helping me?"

Greisch smiled and said, "Do you have some time?"

"Sure."

He reached into his pocket and took out his cell phone. After a few seconds he said, "Hey, Scott. It's Jeff. You're not going to believe who you're having lunch with. Can you meet me at the diner in ten minutes?"

Jeff hung up and said, "Change of plans. We're heading this way."

I was disappointed not to go straight to the files but kept it to myself. Just as we walked up to what was obviously our lunch diner, a blue Ford Explorer turned into the parking lot. The driver tapped his horn and waved.

Greisch led Stanley and me to the car and we waited as the driver got out. He was a tall lanky guy, about the same age as Greisch and me.

The man, presumably the Scott from the phone conversation, looked at me with the same quizzical look I must have had.

Greisch was enjoying the drama. Finally he said, "Scott McCallum, I'd like you to meet Phil Osgood."

McCallum's eyes widened. He looked at Greisch, ignoring me. "No shit?"

"No shit."

Both men stood staring at each other in mutual amazement. Then they realized they were leaving me in the dark.

Greisch led. "I'm sorry, Phil. Scott knew Coulon. In fact, in the months before he disappeared, Scott, who is a retired commercial baker, was doing some detective work for him."

Now it was my turn. "No shit?"

They both burst out laughing and simultaneously responded, "No shit."

We spent the next two hours eating grilled cheese sandwiches, drinking coffee and discussing the work Scott and I had done for Coulon. Scott had only worked for him for nine months when he disappeared. But years later, when Emile and Bev's bodies were found and it came out that I had been duped into doing work that was the basis for some of Coulon's blackmail, Scott realized that he might have been in the same position. He contacted the FBI and told them his story.

I couldn't believe what I was hearing or how incredibly decent the man I was listening to was.

"Scott, I think you might be part of the reason I'm not in jail right now. A big part."

Jeff smiled at Scott. They shared a laugh.

I looked at them both. "What?"

Greisch spoke first. "A week after your story came out, Scott came to my office and said he thought he had to contact the FBI because he believed your story about being duped."

I turned to Scott. "Why?"

"Because of something that happened just once. One day when Emile was in town, he and I were walking from his office to the parking lot and this incredibly beautiful woman approached us. Emile was giving me instructions on a case and she came up from behind, caught us by surprise. I guess she heard part of our conversation and realized I worked for Emile."

Jeff and I remained quiet, waiting for him to explain.

"Once she greeted us, Emile sent me on my way and discussed whatever it was she wanted to discuss about her case. He almost never let me meet the actual clients. He said it was his company and he wanted to be the one who dealt with the clients. And frankly, that was fine with me. Did he let you meet clients?"

"Eventually he did, with some. But only when he had to. What happened with the lady?"

"A few months later, a week or two after the last time I ever saw Emile, I was in Glencoe, a town just down the road a few miles. I was with my wife. We were walking around town, shopping for something or other. Anyway, that same woman sees me from across the street. I recognized her right away because she was so beautiful, and I guess she recognized me, because she almost ran across the street. I didn't know what to make of it. Then, from about halfway across the street, she starts yelling at me. Calling me a fucking scumbag and every other swear word in the book."

Being the polite man he was, Scott actually lowered his voice when he said 'fucking'.

"What was she upset about?"

"I didn't know. We'd followed her husband. She thought he was cheating – he was. Emile and I caught him on camera. Emile said he'd deal with her and I figured that was the last I'd hear about it."

"That's how he handled cases like that with me too."

"One of the things she called me was," and here he lowered his voice again, 'a fucking blackmailing shit.'"

"Wow. If she knew, the husband must have told her. He must not have been willing to be blackmailed."

"That's what I thought too, but not until years later, after your story came out."

"What did you do afterwards? After the lady yelled at you?"

"First I tried to explain to my wife what the hell had just happened."

Jeff and I both laughed at that.

"Then I tried to contact Emile to get him to explain. But I never saw him again."

"Did you ever hear from the woman or her husband?"

"No, but I told the story to the FBI. I don't know if they tracked her down or not. That was after I read about you. I contacted them and they took my statement. Then, a few days later, I was contacted by some agents from out your way. I told them the same story and admitted that I might have been doing the same thing you were doing for Coulon and that I also didn't know I was doing anything illegal. And I told them I didn't know what the woman meant until I learned about you."

"That took a lot of guts, Scott. Thank you."

"You're welcome."

We spent the next hour discussing how I discovered that Emile had been using me to blackmail him. When I explained that I had gone through every case I could remember to try to see if the parties might have been blackmailable, Greisch perked up.

"We can do the same thing here. I've got some of Coulon's files in the basement of his old office."

"I'd be surprised if he left anything that sensitive behind, but it's worth a look. Thank you."

Scott was sort of giving me a look. I could tell he wanted in, desperately.

"Would you be interested in looking at them too? Your local knowledge would be really helpful."

"I was hoping you'd ask."

Jeff laughed out loud.

"Yeah, I think he got that, Scott."

For two days, Scott and I went through Coulon's Winnetka files in my hotel room. If there was a single huge Chicago client, 'the big one' that Emile often mentioned, we couldn't tell who it was. We sorted the clients we did know about by how blackmailable we perceived them to be and contacted those we found most probable. No one admitted to having been blackmailed.

A couple of files did catch my eye. The first was a corporate client, a legitimate marijuana producer called Dominion Products. Dominion was actively trying to get pot legalized in states across the country, including Illinois. According to Emile's notes, a Dominion executive named Jim Burley hired him to try to get dirt on three state officials who were strongly opposed to the legalization. Two were state senators and one was a state representative.

Two of the files were thin, but one, on a state senator named Deirdre White, was full of information. White was part of an Illinois political family that rivaled the Daley's. Her father was a sitting US senator, and it was widely assumed that Deirdre would eventually move from Springfield to Washington and take over her father's seat.

Emile's file on White was filled with newspaper articles outlining her cozy relationships with executives and lobbyists from industries ranging from meat producers to agricultural commodity producers to chemical companies to the gun lobby. She was clearly someone who could be bought. With Dominion's deep pockets, I wondered why they didn't just write her a check the way everyone else did. I found the answer deeper in the file. White's brother had died from a drug overdose. Dominion was fighting this unscrupulous politician on the one issue about which she had any sense of decency. And in the spirit of most American politicians, she portrayed herself as her constituents' one true moral crusader. The conservative news media ate it up and gave her all the coverage she could dream of.

And that's where the file ended. If there had been more, the Feds would probably have kept the White file, but since the information in the file was all public, they apparently weren't worried about it.

But Scott had helped Emile investigate White. Emile told Scott that since she couldn't be bought by Dominion, they had to find some other dirt on her. And they did. Illinois' primary opponent to legalized marijuana, the moral crusader who portrayed pot as a gateway drug and regularly and publicly shed tears describing her brother's doomed struggle, had a heroin habit of her own.

As with many of his cases, Emile didn't need to catch her red handed to blackmail her, but in her case, he came close.

Senator Deirdre White fired a staffer, Sally Harrington, in a public fit of rage. According to Harrington, the senator almost immediately saw the stupidity of the firing and called her the next day. She apologized and told her she could have her job back, but Harrington wouldn't have any of it. When she refused the offer, White went apeshit for a second time, telling her she'd never work in politics again.

Perhaps out of survival instinct, Harrington never disclosed what she had done to make White so angry. Nonetheless the story piqued Emile's interest. He tracked Harrington down and found her working as an administrator at a title company in a small town outside of Champaign. True to her spiteful word, White had got her blackballed from Springfield to Washington.

130

Emile told Scott that when he met with Harrington, he told her he was representing Dominion Products and that he was investigating Senator White. Harrington, who Coulon described as frustrated and bitter, scoffed when he mentioned White's strong feelings against legalizing weed. He asked what she meant and she apparently looked at Coulon and mimicked shooting a needle into her left arm. She never said a word.

It didn't matter. Now Emile knew where to dig.

For the next few weeks, sometimes with Scott's help, he tailed White. Scott said that on the days he'd helped Emile tail White, they hadn't seen her doing anything untoward. But he'd only helped on a couple of afternoons. Emile may have found more. And knowing what we now knew, Scott and I felt that Emile might have been able to blackmail her without concrete evidence.

I tried to contact Sally Harrington. The first thing I learned was that her relationship with the White's had been restored. She had moved from rural Illinois to Washington, DC and was working as a legislative assistant to none other than Deirdre's father, US Senator Daniel White. Harrington took my call, but as soon as I started to question her about her former employer, State Senator Deirdre White, she politely rung off.

Six months after Emile disappeared, State Senator White made a public announcement that she was checking into rehab, portraying herself as an innocent victim of big pharma. Apparently her habit was so bad that she couldn't hide it. Not surprisingly, all these years later she still held her senate seat.

Along with the outburst by the beautiful woman to McCallum and his wife on the streets of Glencoe, the White file seemed to confirm that Emile was at least trying to replicate his Connecticut blackmailing practices in Illinois.

But that information didn't get me any closer to finding out what happened to him.

Scott and I did find one other interesting bit of information in Emile's Winnetka files. In 2007 and 2008, Emile had been doing a fair amount of work with a Chicago law firm called Richardson, Milton & Oats. That work ended in November of '08. It was all before Scott worked for Emile, so he didn't know anything about the work or why it ended.

I talked with a couple of lawyers there and was eventually directed to one of the firm's partners, a nice man in his early sixties who had actually worked with Emile and knew he was dead. He explained that the firm stopped working with Emile because one of their cleaning ladies told them Coulon had offered to pay her to copy files. He'd questioned Emile about it, but didn't believe his answers and simply stopped working with him.

When I heard that I immediately thought of the similar incident that had played out in Greenwich years earlier, when I'd bumped into the man I'd occasionally seen in Emile's office, running a cleaning crew at Fort & Clarence. I decided to investigate him when I got back to Connecticut.

After a week of productive work and many heartfelt laughs in Winnetka, I said goodbye to Scott, Jeff and Stanley, the pirate dog, and headed back to Connecticut.

Chapter 28:

As far as I knew the police weren't making much progress on solving the murders. Canadian authorities did establish that Emile and Bev entered Canada on October 29, 2012. They crossed the border near Stanstead, Quebec, south of Sherbrooke. That was the last known trace of them until their bodies were found years later. If they stayed in a hotel or ate or bought gas anywhere between Stanstead and Muskoka, the police couldn't prove it.

I decided to pursue the only open lead I could think of – the cleaning guy in Greenwich.

I contacted the lawyer I'd worked with the night I'd bumped into him, Patty Mahoney. She agreed to meet me for a drink.

We met at 8pm at a restaurant at the top of Greenwich Avenue, near where I'd settled things with Hendrie a few months earlier.

Without naming names, I gave her some general background on Emile's blackmail schemes and my unwitting participation. I also told her about the bodies, my two trips to Muskoka and Coulon's Chicago operations. She knew a lot of the background from what she'd read in the papers and online, but I gave her more detail. Finally, I told her what I suspected about the cleaning crew her firm had employed. She obviously wouldn't mention specific cases but said there had been two occasions when her opposition seemed to have information she'd thought was confidential. She'd actually wondered if someone was stealing information from her files. She remembered the cases and said she'd look up their dates and find out what company was cleaning her firm's offices on those dates.

Three days later she called and said that a firm called Spotless Cleaners had been cleaning her firm's offices during that time period. She didn't know why, but they'd stopped using them a few years later. As we spoke, I googled Spotless. It only took me a few clicks to find their website. I opened the site and found pictures of the staff. The first man pictured was the guy I'd seen at Patty's office and with Bev at Emile's office. I recognized him immediately. His name was Stavros Gavris. He was the owner. Spotless was based in Mount Kisco, New York, twenty minutes from Greenwich.

Given what Patty said about her opponents' access to privileged information, we concluded it was possible that Emile was paying Spotless, or at least Gavris, to search lawyers' desks and files for useful information.

The next morning I called the number on the website and asked to speak to Stavros. The woman who answered said Stavros hadn't been running the firm for a few years, that his son had taken over. I asked if I could talk to him and she told me he was on site somewhere, but that she'd pass along my information.

The son, Michael Gavris, called me back ninety minutes later.

"Mr. Gavris, my name is Philip Osgood. I'm trying to get in touch with your father."

"What's this about?" His voice was curt and defensive.

"I just wanted to ask him some questions."

"Look, mister, I don't know who you are or what you're up to, but my father's been missing for six years."

I did the math. He disappeared in 2012, the same year Emile and Bev did. I softened my tone. "I'm sorry. I didn't know. What happened?"

He ignored my question. "Who are you?"

I considered how to answer. "I'm looking into some events that took place in 2012. Was that around the time he disappeared?"

"Yes."

"Could I meet with you? Today? Now if you can?"

"Why, what do you want?"

"I think we might be able to help each other."

We met in the parking lot outside of a coffee shop in Mount Kisco that afternoon. I got there early and bought two black coffees. Gavris pulled in driving a new Spotless Cleaners service van.

As he stepped out of the van his appearance surprised me. The guy was another ball of muscle, smaller but more jacked than Farro.

I got out of my car and approached him.

"Hi, Mr. Gavris. I'm Phil Osgood. Thank you for seeing me." I extended my hand and braced myself for the crush. But he shook it normally, even tentatively, clearly worried.

"I got us some coffees. We could sit inside the shop, but it might be better to talk in one of our cars."

He pointed at my Jeep Cherokee and we each got in.

"So who are you? Why do you want to know about my father?"

I suspected that he must have googled me and learned I was linked to the murder of Emile and Bev. I didn't know if he was aware they were his father's former associates. At any rate I humored him.

"I used to work for a man named Emile Coulon. I believe he and your father occasionally worked together."

His expression didn't change and he didn't respond.

"As you may know, Emile Coulon was a private investigator in Greenwich. He and his associate, Beverly Sutton, disappeared about the same time your father did."

He still gave me nothing. "And as I suspect you know, if you googled me before this meeting, a few months ago their bodies were found buried at a cottage north of Toronto."

Finally, he spoke. "Yeah. And so far as I can tell, you're the prime suspect."

"I was and I may still be, but for whatever it's worth, it wasn't me."

"So what do you want?"

I went with a benign version of the truth.

"In 2009 and early 2010 I saw your father at Coulon's office, a number of times."

"Yeah, so?"

"I was never privy to their business, but Emile's associate, Beverly, told me that your father hired Emile to investigate his brother."

"His brother?"

"As I understand it, they owned Spotless together, and they were having some difficulties."

"That's just bullshit." Gavris paused for a moment. "He doesn't have a brother."

"What?" I sounded more surprised than I actually was.

"My father has two sisters and neither one is involved in the business. They don't even live around here."

My mind was racing. Michael Gavris was getting impatient.

"What the fuck is going on? Why are you investigating my father?"

I considered my answer for a moment.

"As you probably know, Coulon was using the information he gathered on his clients, some of which I unwittingly gathered for him, to blackmail them."

Gavris grunted his assent.

"I suspect his dishonesty wasn't limited to blackmail."

Gavris grunted again. "And?" he demanded.

"I think he may have found ways to steal sensitive information and sell it."

Gavris was looking increasingly uneasy. I had no idea if he was doing the same shit I suspected his father had done.

"How do you think this relates to my father? Are you saying you think he was involved?"

I nodded.

"Why?"

"One night in 2010 I was meeting with a lawyer at her firm. I saw your father there, running his cleaning crew."

"Yeah, so?"

"It was odd because I had seen him in Coulon's offices several times before that. I mentioned it to Coulon's assistant, Bev, and eventually to Coulon. They told me the story about your father wanting his 'brother' investigated."

"So a blackmailer and his lying partner lied to you. How does that implicate my father?"

"I always felt they were lying to me about their relationship with your father, even before you confirmed it just now. So I looked into it."

"What do you mean? How?"

"I spoke to some people at the law firm where I saw him cleaning and they said they felt that someone might have been stealing sensitive information during the time Spotless was working for them. They didn't suspect Spotless but when I asked a lawyer there about it, she did some checking and confirmed that the suspicious exposure of private information occurred during the time your father's firm was cleaning for them."

Gavris looked understandably pissed.

"So you're telling our customers that we're stealing information from them? Fuck you. We're not and never would."

"I'm not telling customers. I spoke to one person at one firm. A former customer. They stopped using you a few years ago."

"Fuck."

He looked angry, but also appeared to be grappling with something.

"Look, I'm not accusing you of anything. This all happened a long time ago."

"That doesn't matter. If this bullshit gets out, my business will be fucking crushed."

"There's no reason it will. If you're not doing the same things your father was doing – might have been doing – this will never get out."

Even as I said it, I knew it probably wasn't true, but there was nothing I could do about it.

"Bullshit."

We sat there, both silent. I figured that if he didn't think there was some possibility that what I was saying was true, he'd have either punched me or left.

He stayed.

"Do you think it's possible?"

He glared at me.

"It could be an explanation for his disappearance. Do you have any other theories?"

We sat there, quietly. After almost a minute he said, "It's possible."

He opened up a bit, so I nudged him along.

"What do you know about his disappearance? Did anything peculiar happen in the weeks or months before?"

"Not really. He was always going away for a day or two, sometimes longer."

"What do you mean?"

"My parents are divorced. They had been for years when he disappeared. My father liked women. There were lots of them. And he was always going off with them for long weekends or whatever."

"Is that what happened in 2012?"

"I don't know. Maybe. When he first left that's what I thought. He told me he was going to be out of town for a few days. Told me to run things. It happened a lot and I didn't ask questions. I didn't want to know about his women."

"When did you become concerned?"

"After three or four days, I called him. To see when he was coming back. He never answered. The calls went straight to voice mail."

"Did you call the police?"

"Yeah, after about a week. The Mount Kisco police investigated his disappearance, but never found anything."

"Really? Nothing?"

"Nope. Nothing of significance."

"No credit card records after his disappearance? No phone records?"

"Nothing on his credit card. The last thing on his phone was a call to a woman he was seeing back here. Apparently not the one he went away with."

"Who did he go away with? Was she reported missing?"

"I don't know."

"Do you know where he called from?"

"Yeah, up around Albany."

"And nothing else?"

"Nothing."

"Why wasn't there more of an investigation?"

Gavris looked at me. His demeanor changed. It softened. He looked lost.

"My father wasn't the most honest man. I think the police think he got in over his head on something and simply took off. If something worse happened, they didn't seem too concerned."

"What do you think?"

"To be honest sometimes I think he's dead and other times I think he's going to show up at my door with some stupid woman on his arm and a fistful of cash."

Chapter 29:

While the media's interest in the murders quickly faded, my life seemed forever changed. I'd always been viewed as a decent man, an honest man. Now I wasn't. I'd gotten a real thrill out of doing some seedy investigations, but my dark side didn't run so deep that I liked being viewed as even a little bit dirty or dishonest. It wasn't who I was and it wasn't who I wanted my sons to think I was. They believed in my innocence but knew I'd allowed myself to get involved in something illegal, unwittingly but nonetheless fully involved. I was ashamed I'd been so stupid. Ultimately, the person who made me look stupid, who intentionally used me to do his illegal legwork, was Emile. And he was dead. I don't know why I felt finding his killer would somehow vindicate me, but I did. I had to find him.

Eventually my obsession impacted my marriage. I'd failed to see how difficult it all was on Jenny. While her immediate circle of female friends remained wonderfully supportive, the rest of our community was less kind. Every time she went out, she encountered stares and muffled conversations. She was left out of events she normally would have led and dropped from boards and committees on which she served. She even lost her part-time job working for a florist.

She was fed up. My interest in 'detecting' got us into this mess and my obsession with finding the truth was more than she could take. She didn't officially leave me, but one day I came home and found a note. She decided to go stay with her sister in Boston and wasn't sure when she was coming back.

I was devastated. We'd been together since college. We'd built a life together, raised children together, raised a rooftop satellite together. There was no part of my adult life not entwined with Jenny. I couldn't imagine my life without her.

But she'd married a young man with a promising future, a bond trader, a hedge fund manager, not a guy whose life was a tangle of murder, blackmail, thugs and social exile. She hadn't signed up for that. I wanted to blame Emile, to think she was another thing he'd taken from me. And that was true, in part. But if I'd been satisfied to stay in my own cushy lane, none of it would have happened. It was on me.

That should have been enough to make me walk away. But I didn't see how I could.

Jenny had been the one person who truly believed in me. From the early days of our relationship, I could see it in the way she looked at me, the way she smiled at me. Ever since I discovered that Emile had used me, that he'd outsmarted me, I knew she saw me differently.

That look was gone. Her belief in me was gone. Emile had taken that from me. I had to get it back. In my obsessed, devastated mind the only way to do that was to find out who killed Emile and Bev. Nothing else mattered.

Chapter 30:

Stavros Gavris of Spotless Cleaners was the only slightly hopeful lead I had. I focused on him.

He disappeared on October 29, 2012 – the same day that Emile and Bev were last seen, the day they crossed the border into Canada.

I called Detective Jim Houston of the Ontario Provincial Police. After I explained what I suspected about Gavris and the fact that he disappeared on the exact day that Emile and Bev were last seen, Houston agreed to look into it.

A few days later he called me back. Immigration records showed Gavris had entered Canada on a train from New York to Montreal on the 29th, about four hours ahead of Emile and Bev.

His trail dried up after that. There was no record of him leaving Canada.

Chapter 31:

While I was trying to figure out the implications of my discoveries regarding Gavris, Scott McCallum, Emile's Chicago stooge, was working on the case from a different angle. The whole thing really ate at him. He didn't like to feel stupid any more than I did. He couldn't let it go either. He did everything he could to find more information about Coulon's activities in Chicago.

His breakthrough came on a golf course on a Tuesday morning. He called me from the parking lot as soon as he finished his round.

"Phil, it's Scott McCallum. From Chicago."

"Hi, Scott. You're the man who kept me out of jail. I'll never forget your name."

"Hah. Well, let's see how you feel after you hear what I have to tell you. It might lead to a lot of trouble. For you."

"Uh-oh."

"I've got a hunch. I just finished golfing with three buddies. I'm sitting in my car with my golf shoes still on."

I chuckled, but his urgency had my full attention.

"While we were out on the course, we were talking about new ownership groups trying to buy the Cubs. Who knows if they're even for sale, but you know how rumors go on things like that. Anyway, we were talking about different groups and someone mentioned that Harlan Alversen was trying to put together a bid."

"Who's Harlan Alversen?"

"He's one of the richest guys in Chicago. His father or grandfather started a huge shipping company. After his father died, Alversen was the sole heir. He's worth like seven or eight billion."

"Alversen Shipping?"

"Yes."

"How does that tie into any of this?"

"When Harlan's name was mentioned, another guy in the foursome said 'Alversen would never be allowed to bid on the Cubs, let alone buy them.' That caught me by surprise so I asked why and he said there were rumors that he was a pedophile."

My mind jumped to the obvious conclusion. "Do you think Coulon was blackmailing Alversen?"

"Maybe."

"Why? Was there any connection?"

"Okay, this is a big stretch, but one day I saw a note on Emile's desk. It had Alversen's name and a telephone number."

"Did you ask him about it?"

"I did but he blew me off. Said he was calling him to follow up a lead on someone else or some bullshit."

"A name on a desk is a long way from proof."

"I know, Phil. I may be grasping at straws, but something about this seems plausible to me."

"Why?"

"Apparently Alversen's always had the reputation of being a really bad guy. If Emile got wind of anything about Alversen's activities with minors, and from what I heard today it wasn't fifteen-year-olds, he might have followed him. If he found enough to go after him, he could have asked for millions. Enough to never have to work again."

He paused to let that all sink in.

I responded, "Or enough to be killed for."

"Exactly."

"Any idea how we can find out more?"

"I do. Do you have a tux?"

Chapter 32:

Two days later I was in Chicago. McCallum was invited to a fundraiser for some local cause and I was his guest. Harlan Alversen was one of the chairs of the event. Our plan, my plan, was to get a moment alone with him and drop Coulon's name to catch his reaction.

Unfortunately, it turns out that even if you're in the same room, getting a word in with a billionaire isn't as easy as you might think. The closest I got to being 'alone' with him was when I edged my way into a group of nine or ten people, all circled around him, hanging on his every word and trying to get their moment with him.

As the alleged pedophile was leaving our little group to grace another, he passed me. I figured I'd take my shot.

As he passed I said, "Excuse me, Mr. Alversen?"

Still walking, he turned and smiled.

"Emile Coulon asked me to send his regards."

I watched his eyes. There was a flash of confusion, then recognition, then nothing. He kept walking and I kept watching. He went from the group I was standing with to another and stayed with it. If he was distracted, I couldn't tell. I stayed close enough that he could find me if he wanted to, and within his line of sight. He didn't look my way.

Scott was standing in another group. He watched Alversen while he pretended to be listening to a conversation.

After a few minutes, Alversen signaled someone. Seconds later an attractive young woman approached him and they exchanged a few personal words. Almost every man in the room was wearing a tuxedo or a dark suit. I looked around and saw a middle-aged, slightly overweight woman in a tight-fitting, bright red dress. I stood next to her, to give Alversen a reference point. After speaking with the young woman for a moment

Alversen glanced in my direction. Thirty seconds later, his associate did.

I struck up a conversation with the woman in the red dress and Scott discreetly followed the young woman, Alversen's associate. He later told me that she talked to a few other people in the room and discreetly pointed at me. Each person she spoke with looked in my direction, but no one recognized me. One of them, a handsome 6'3" kid in his twenties made his way in my direction and struck up a conversation with my friend in the red dress, Susan something, and me. Scott passed behind him and gave me a nod.

The young man extended his hand to Susan.

"Hi. I'm Frank Tanzy." He smiled at her.

Susan's interest in me seemed to wane. She introduced herself but, to her tall new friend's disappointment, didn't introduce me.

After chatting with her for the shortest possible time, he tried to bring me into the conversation.

"I'm sorry, sir. I didn't mean to interrupt you and Susan."

I just smiled. Even though I wanted him to know my name to give it to Alversen, I decided to make him earn it.

Frustrated by my lack of response, he extended his hand. "Frank Tanzy. How are you?"

I shook his hand. "Well, thanks."

Before he could ask my name, I said, "Susan and I were just saying what a nice event this is, and what a great cause. Weren't we, Susan?"

Glad that I was directing the handsome young man's attention back to her, Susan jumped right back in. She didn't stop talking or touching his arm for a solid minute. I was enjoying his anguish and pretended to scan the room, as if I was going to move on from the two of them.

Finally, she paused and in a serious non sequitur Frank turned to me and asked, "Are you from Chicago?"

"No."

He looked so frustrated I tried not to laugh. To his surprise and Susan's, I followed up with, "My name is Phil Osgood. You can tell Alversen I'm staying at the Ambassador until the day after tomorrow."

Before he could respond I turned to walk away.

"Night, Frank. Nice to meet you, Susan."

The next day at 2pm the phone in my hotel room rang. The caller didn't tell me his name. He simply told me to meet him on the northern most dock in Diversey Harbor that night, at 7:45. He hung up before I could respond.

I didn't recognize the voice but felt sure it was Alversen or one of his minions.

The meeting seemed risky. If Alversen was the man who ordered Emile and Bev's death, adding me to the list wouldn't bother him. But I wasn't entirely convinced. I kept coming back to the issue of me. Why frame me? What did I have to do with the blackmailing of a guy in Chicago? And why would Alversen lure Emile and Bev to Canada instead of just dumping their bodies in the water here? It would have been a hell of a lot easier.

The meeting was a lead. I decided to go.

Chapter 33:

Diversey Harbor is a busy boat basin in Lincoln Park on the north side of Chicago, just off Lake Michigan. There are fifteen or so docks in the harbor, spanning from the inland side out toward the lake side. The longest docks are at the north end. I cautiously made my way to the northern most one, where we were supposed to meet. It was across from the outlet to the lake.

The harbor wasn't busy, but there was activity. People were scattered over the dozen or so docks, cleaning and securing boats, drinking, partying and eating late suppers. Some were still plodding their way in from the lake. I felt safe.

I made my way down the last dock. I purposefully scanned each boat and tried to make eye contact with everyone I saw. No one seemed to be waiting for me.

Near the end of the dock, I stopped and looked south toward Chicago's skyline. I checked the nearest docks. No one appeared to be watching me. I looked east across the water. Lakeshore Drive, which ran between the harbor and Lake Michigan, was at a standstill with bumper-to-bumper traffic in both directions.

It was almost dusk. A boat emerged from an underpass, puttering in towards the docks. There didn't seem to be anyone driving or even on board.

Then a head popped up.

I saw a flash. And another. Something pierced my chest. Then my neck. Gunshots.

The impact pushed me back and to my right. My hands moved to the pain. My legs tangled and gave way. I stumbled and fell face first into the lake.

Chapter 34:

I woke up in a strange room, a hospital room. There was some-one there. A nurse. After a minute she looked at me. She looked a little surprised to see my eyes open – not a reassuring feeling.

"Well, hello. How are you?"

I tried to speak but couldn't. There was a tube down my throat and bandages surrounding my neck. I moved my hands, my feet.

"Don't worry. You're fine. You won't be able to talk for a few days, but ..."

The next day or two were blurs of semi-consciousness. I think I saw Jenny and the boys a few times. By the third day I was fairly cogent and happy to realize that at some point I'd been de-intubated.

My youngest son, who looked exhausted, was there when I woke up. He got Jenny and his brothers. I could see the relief on all their faces.

Before they could explain what had happened, police offi-cers questioned me. The doctors didn't want me to speak for a few days, so my son Mike gave me his iPad to peck out answers and my own questions. I told the officers about the phone call and the planned meeting with Alversen. I described walking to the end of the dock. Everything was surprisingly clear in my mind. I remembered seeing a white, open-bowed speed-boat coming slowly in from the lake, through the Lakeshore Drive underpass. And seeing muzzle flashes. I wasn't sure if they came from the boat or the underpass behind it.

And that was it. I couldn't remember anything else.

The officers questioned me for another forty minutes, mostly trying to establish who else knew about my meeting with Alversen. I assured them that, aside from whoever Al-versen told, only Scott McCallum and I knew about it. And just before I was shot, I'd seen Scott on my side of the harbor in the parking lot behind me. By land the underpass was a mile away. Usain Bolt couldn't have made it to the underpass or the boat in time to shoot me.

After the detectives left, my family answered my questions. They explained that seconds after I was shot a woman named Margaret Shoshanna jumped from her boat into the lake to save me. Supporting my statement to the police, they said that Scott ran from the parking lot when he heard the shots, but that it was Ms. Shoshanna who saved me. They all smiled when they talked about her. There was clearly more to the story, but when I pressed them, as best one could through an iPad, they said it was her story to tell.

They did explain that my shooting was national news. The combination of a murder and blackmail suspect being shot, possibly by a billionaire or his people, and then 'spectacularly' rescued, caught the country's attention. I had to wait a day to learn just what they meant.

The next morning the boys entered my room smiling and giddy with excitement. Jenny followed close behind, shepherding a woman. Jenny spoke first.

"Phil, this is Ms. Shoshanna. Margaret. She saved you. You literally owe her your life."

I tried to sit up, but still couldn't. Margaret, kind soul that she was, made her way to me – again.

She was in her early thirties, about 5'3" with a beautiful, happy face, kind brown eyes and a smile that lit up the room. She weighed about two-hundred and fifty pounds.

I extended my hand and she took it. I squeezed and gently pulled her a little closer. My first spoken words since the shooting were for her.

I whispered, "Thank you."

She teared up and then I teared up.

My third son Chris said, "Margaret, you have to tell him the story. He's been trying to get it out of us, but you have to tell him. Please."

Margaret's naturally rosy cheeks turned a brighter shade of red.

I pecked onto the iPad, pleading, "What?"

She laughed and shook her head. It was clear that my family had spent some time with her and that they were all terribly fond of her.

I pecked again. "What happened?"

I looked from Margaret to Jenny and the boys. They all looked back to her.

Margaret burst out laughing. "You guys are the worst. I can't believe you're making me tell him."

She looked from me to my family to a pile of newspapers on the window ledge of my room. She nodded to my son Jay and said, "Do you have the Sun Times in that stack?"

He feathered through a massive stack of papers and, without letting me see anything, handed Margaret what I presumed was the Chicago Sun Times. She unfolded it and turned back to me. She held up the paper. The front page was a full-page cover picture with the headline "Our Margaret".

I looked from the headline to the picture. It was Margaret in the water, swimming sidestroke and holding me. The right back side of her body, from her head to her toes, was just above water and clearly visible. She appeared to be naked.

No one in the room spoke. Everyone watched as my eyes left the paper and met hers. My eyes asked the question and she simply nodded. That was enough. Everyone erupted in laughter. Our normally nice nurse rushed in and tried to quiet everyone down, but when she saw Margaret, she shook her hand and started to laugh too.

Ignoring them all I rasped, "What happened?" My obvious confusion made them laugh harder, even Margaret.

Finally, she took pity on me. "I'd been out on the lake on our boat with my parents. We'd just come in from a day on the water. We have the last slip on the south side of the dock you were on, right by where you fell in."

I tried to picture her boat but couldn't.

"My mom and dad were heading to the car and I was below, in the little cabin, changing my clothes. At the exact worse possible moment for me, when I didn't have a stitch on, I heard what sounded like a couple of rifle shots. I looked out the tiny window and saw you fall into the water."

At this point everyone's laughter had turned into quiet awe. Margaret didn't seem comfortable being the heroine she was but went on. "I grabbed a towel and ran for the back of the boat. You were floating face down and drifting out."

I tried to remember but again couldn't.

"I dove off the side of the boat and swam a few strokes to you. Along the way I guess I somehow lost my towel."

She was content to leave it there, but my children wouldn't let her.

"As I said, you were face down. When I got to you, I turned you onto your back and supported your head, keeping it above water. Your neck was gushing blood. I swam us a few strokes, back to my errant towel, and held it to your neck."

Chris said, "Margaret, you were amazing." Everyone else chimed in.

She went on, "By then there were two other people on the dock. It was three feet above the water level, too high, so I swam you over to the swimming platform of my dad's boat and we lifted you out there. Other people got some fresh towels and held them to your wounds until the ambulance came. You had lots of people helping you that day."

I took her hand and squeezed.

Jenny put a hand on Margaret's shoulder. "Margaret's been

through a lot, Phil. There are a lot of pictures out there. The one you saw is less intrusive than most of the others."

"I'm so sorry," I whispered.

She wouldn't have any more of it. She went on, "There is some good that's come of this, beyond you surviving I mean." She smiled her beautiful smile and patted my hand. "Once the press got word that you were on the dock to meet with Alversen, he became the prime suspect. And the hushed rumors about him being a pedophile have been made very, very public. Even if he isn't responsible for your shooting, he's ruined. Hopefully on his way to jail for a very long time."

I pecked furiously at the iPad. "Was it him? Did he shoot me? Or his goons?"

Jenny answered that one.

"We don't know. It definitely wasn't him. He has a solid alibi. It might not have been ordered by him either. There are a lot of us who'd like to kill you, Phil."

The boys all groaned. She looked at them. "Too soon?"

Chapter 35:

Fortunately, my wounds weren't as bad they first seemed. Ten days after I regained consciousness, I was released from the hospital. My doctors told me I shouldn't fly and I didn't think I could take a fifteen-hour car ride, so I rented a two-bedroom Airbnb in Chicago, a couple of blocks from the hospital.

Jenny stayed around to help but slept in a different room. That alone created a fair amount of tension. The fact that I'd been shot seemed to both irritate her and vindicate her position that I should have given up the whole detecting bullshit years ago. I could hardly argue. But she seemed not to understand how much getting shot actually hurt. After a week, I encouraged her to head home. I made the case that I spent most of my time seeing doctors, going to physical therapy and sleeping, so I didn't really need help. But we both knew that was just a cover story; two boxes of my files from Connecticut had arrived.

After she left, I brooded, feeling alone and abandoned. I couldn't focus on the case with her around and I couldn't focus on it without her around. I was having trouble caring about much of anything.

On the third day my cell phone rang. It was Margaret. She asked if she could come see me. I was wallowing in self-pity and tried to put her off, but she wouldn't have it.

An hour later she was at my door. She came bearing gifts in the form of cookies and a murder mystery. While I admonished her for bringing me gifts, I appreciated her kindness.

I showed her to the living room of my little apartment.

"Phil, I've been reading up on you. You've had quite an interesting twenty years."

I smiled a mocking smile. "Nah. Just another bond trader. I've read a lot about you too, in the papers and online. The whole city is beaming with pride over you, Margaret."

"My friends call me Maggie."

"So tell me, Maggie, what do you do?" And I paused and smiled when I said her name. "The papers say you're some sort of analyst, but it's all pretty vague."

"Yeah. I'm trying not to let all of this attention ruin my job. I write and do research for a liberal think tank. My work is outward facing to a small group of business and government leaders. I research and interpret data."

"That sounds intriguingly vague."

She just laughed.

"I do have another interest. A passion really."

"What's that?"

"Detective work."

"Oh shit."

We both started to laugh, which hurt like hell. She saw me wince and tried to stop laughing, but that only made it worse.

"I was thinking maybe I could help you."

"Not a chance."

"Why not?"

I gave her a look and pointed to my neck and my chest.

"I don't want to be in the field, Phil." She chuckled. "I'll leave that to you. But let me help you behind the scenes, doing research. It's what I do and I'm very good at it."

"Two people I know are dead, Maggie, and I would be too if it wasn't for you. There's no way I'm letting you get involved in this, this shitshow."

"What risk will I be taking? You give me something to research and I'll do it. No one but you and I will ever know."

"No."

"You owe me, Phil." She said it, but there was no power behind it. Maggie didn't mean to play her strong hand. She wasn't that type of person.

"I do. But I'm not going to repay you by putting you in danger. It's not going to happen."

She ignored me.

"So who do you think I should look into first? I was thinking that if you gave me your files on the people you think Coulon blackmailed, I might be able to look at them from a different perspective; be a fresh set of eyes."

"'A fresh set of eyes.' Good God, Maggie, you've been reading too many detective novels."

She looked at the two boxes of files on my dining room table.

"This is better than any novel. This is the real thing. Come on. Let's at least discuss things that are bothering you. Loose ends or unanswered questions."

From the first time I'd met her, I'd sensed a real intelligence in Margaret. And I liked her. She was great company.

I conceded. "Okay. We can discuss things. It would be really helpful if I had someone intelligent to run some pretty farfetched ideas by. But it's just between us. I don't want you doing anything 'outward facing' to use your words. No danger."

"That's fine. I won't meet anyone face to face but let me make calls to follow leads. Just calls. I'll buy a few burner phones to use for research. No one on the outside will know my identity."

"Burner phones. Listen to you."

She grinned at me. I could feel my mood lifting.

For the next few hours we discussed the case from my first job with Emile to discovering he and Bev were sometimes lovers to their disappearances and deaths. I told her about Senator Rawlings and the other people whom Emile had blackmailed – or at least the ones I knew about. I explained my angst about Hendrie and how I had made things right with him by virtue of the statute of limitations. And I told her about turning myself in.

She asked about Chicago and I told her about Emile's 'big client', who I believed was a bigger-than-big target for blackmail, most likely Alversen. I told her about McCallum, whom she'd met, and how Emile had used Scott in the same way he'd used me. I told her that Scott had seen Alversen's name on Emile's desk, and how we'd baited him.

I explained that aside from Alversen and his people, only Scott knew about the Diversey Harbor meeting. I trusted Scott implicitly. Alversen had to be responsible for my shooting. He was the only one who would have had time to set it up. If he tried to kill me for just mentioning Coulon's name, he had to be the prime suspect in Bev and Emile's deaths.

Somehow, I had to tie him to them.

I told her about Stavros Gavris possibly stealing information from Fort & Clarence and how he'd traveled to Canada the same day that Emile and Bev had. I explained that I tried to tie Gavris to blackmail victims but had come up empty. Still, his presence in Canada at the time of the murders raised a lot of questions.

We ordered dinner and Maggie went out and got some wine and Diet Coke.

Over dinner we discussed the shooting.

"Did you know I was the only person who actually saw the muzzle flashes?"

"I wondered about that. I heard the shots from the cabin of my parents' boat, but I wasn't in a position to see the flashes."

"A number of other people heard them too but until I regained consciousness, no one had been able to tell the police precisely where the shots came from. It was weird because I was looking at the boat, watching it putter across the harbor. At first, I didn't think there was anyone in it."

"What do you mean?"

"There wasn't anyone at the helm. I thought it was idling, drifting from the underpass. I didn't think anyone was on-board. Then, just before I was shot, I saw someone. A head popped up from the open cockpit."

"Did that person have a rifle?"

"I don't know. He was facing me and I saw the flashes, but I never saw a rifle."

"My parents know the guy who owns that boat."

"They do?"

"Yeah. He keeps it one dock down from ours, has for years."

"Could it be him?"

"No. He's in his seventies. I doubt he could see you from a hundred yards, let alone shoot you from a moving boat."

"Why did he leave the helm?"

"He was putting on his bumpers."

"How do you know?"

"Are you kidding? Everyone on the dock knows every detail, including my parents. He cleared the underpass, turned toward his dock, put his boat in neutral and put on his bumpers as he idled forward. Lots of boaters here do the same thing when they're alone."

"But he wasn't at the side of the boat. I saw his head pop up."

"He was getting the bumpers from a storage compartment under the back seat."

"Hmm."

"It wasn't him, Phil. He's a nice old guy."

"The police seem to agree with you. They cleared him."

"I know."

"So the working assumption is that whoever shot me was in the underpass on the narrow footpath that runs along the northern side. They think he came in from the lake side, shot me from the cover of the underpass and then went back out the same way."

She nodded. "I read that divers found a rifle on the lakebed on the north side of the underpass, but the police haven't been able to trace its ownership."

"They did confirm it was the rifle that shot me."

We cleared the table and started putting the dishes in the dishwasher.

"Whoever shot you had to know you were going to be on that dock at that time. Right?"

"Definitely. I'd only been on the dock for a minute or two when it happened. Even if someone else was following me, they wouldn't have had time to get across the harbor and Lakeshore and back under the underpass to shoot me."

"Everything points to Alversen."

"Or someone acting on his behalf."

"But Alversen claims he didn't know about the meeting. He says he never called me at my hotel or anywhere else."

"I know."

"But's he's the only one who could have known I was going to be on that dock at that time."

"Is he?"

"Scott knew, but I promise you it wasn't him."

"How do you know?"

"I didn't give him advance notice of where we were going. I told him to meet me at my hotel an hour before I was supposed to meet Alversen. We took a cab from the hotel up to the harbor. Until I told the cab driver to take us to Diversey Harbor, he hadn't a clue."

"Even if someone followed you, there's no way they could have set it all up."

"It had to be Alversen or one of his guys."

Maggie pondered that for a minute. I waited for her to arrive at the same conclusion. Then she said, "Did it?"

"Yes. I was only on the dock for two minutes tops when I got shot. Whoever did it had to know in advance I was going to be there at that time. They needed time to get someone to the underpass."

"I understand that. Whoever called you at the Ambassador shot you. I don't doubt that."

"Are you saying it wasn't Alversen or one of his guys who called?"

"Did it have to be?"

"I told his guy to have him call me there."

"Did the person who called say he was Alversen? Or someone calling on his behalf?"

"I just assumed it was him."

"But what if it was someone else? What if Alversen didn't take the bait?"

"But who else could have known I was staying there?"

"Anyone who wanted to. Hendrie's guys followed you all the way to Canada. How hard would it be..."

"Alright, alright. I get your point."

Maggie smiled her kind smile.

"Anyone who knew I was staying at the Ambassador could have called the hotel, asked for my room and told me to meet them."

That thought did me in. I'd been sure that it had to have been Alversen. The idea that there might be some unknown player still out there was too much. I was exhausted. Maggie and I looked at our phones. It was 11:45. We'd been talking for about ten hours. Maggie ordered an Uber and I walked her downstairs. The car pulled up just as we stepped out.

We hugged goodnight and as she got in, I heard the driver say, "It is you! Hi Margaret!"

She looked out the window at me, grinned broadly and shrugged.

Chapter 36:

Two weeks later I was back in Connecticut.

When I got home, Jenny did everything she could to make me comfortable and to help me with doctors' appointments and physical therapy sessions, but things were awkward between us. I had the impression she'd had enough and wanted to move on. I was so numb I accepted it. Sort of.

I spent as much time as I could away from home, at my office. I focused on my work and gratefully reconnected with my clients. But above everything else, I tried to figure out who shot me.

A week after I got home, Margaret called.

"Are you ready to get back to it?"

"Hello, Maggie."

"Yeah, yeah, enough with the pleasantries. We need to get back to work. What's next?"

"We need to look into Stavros Gavris. He's our best lead."

I knew she was right. For the next few hours we discussed Gavris and what we knew of his movements. He entered Canada on October 29th, 2012 on a train bound for Montreal. Emile and Bev entered the exact same day, by car, crossing the border at a sleepy immigration point seventy miles further east.

I pulled up a map of Quebec on my laptop and expanded it to include Ontario. From where Emile and Bev entered, south of Sherbrooke, it was virtually impossible to drive to Ontario without going through Montreal, where Gavris got off his train. It couldn't have been a coincidence. They must have met there.

But we couldn't prove it.

It bothered us that Gavris had simply disappeared. We were certain that if he wasn't the murderer, he was dead too. But if he was, why wasn't his body in the grave with Emile and Bev?

We tried to build a case for Gavris as the killer, but couldn't really. He had potential motive. Emile had been using him, presumably paying him to steal or copy material from law firms. And Emile was a crook. It was entirely possible that Emile may have skipped town without paying Gavris. It was also conceivable that Gavris had realized Emile was making hundreds of thousands of dollars from the information he'd provided and demanded a bigger cut.

But how could he have lured Emile and Bev to somewhere as remote as Muskoka? If Emile had done something to Gavris, something bad enough to make Gavris want to kill him, there's no way he would have met with him in Montreal or Muskoka. Emile was too smart.

Maybe they had all blackmailed the wrong person and were on the run together. But if that was true, where was Gavris' body?

We weren't getting anywhere. We went back to looking at the blackmail victims.

As far as we could tell, Alversen and Rawlings were Emile's biggest blackmail targets. Maybe I was blinded by the $100 million investment, but I didn't think Rawlings was a murderer. Margaret was more skeptical, but generally agreed.

Alversen was a different story. We both felt he was a sociopath. Anyone who did what he did to children had to be. He had motive and the wherewithal to have Emile and Beverly killed and to set up the elaborate frame in Muskoka. And unlike the Connecticut suspects, at the time of the murder I didn't know about him. So if the bodies were discovered and I came clean about everything, his name wouldn't have come up.

We couldn't place him in Canada at the time of the murders, but chances are he didn't do it himself. Even if he did, he had a cottage on Lake Michigan and could have easily gone in and out of Canada by boat, unnoticed.

But we couldn't tie him to anything. In fact we couldn't tie anyone to anything significant.

The only viable open lead we had was Gavris.

From my perspective, the whole "we" thing was getting out of hand. Maggie was too involved. It was too dangerous.

Chapter 37:

Maggie didn't share my fear. She was fully invested.

When we'd collaborated in Chicago, she sometimes disappeared for days on end for trips or meetings related to her work. After we worked via phone for a few days, she told me she was going to be traveling and would be tied up with some work-related issues for a couple of weeks.

She lied. The day after we spoke, she flew east and quietly settled into a hotel in Greenwich.

Margaret thought that when Emile and Bev and Gavris entered Canada in October of 2012 they'd either been involved in something that had prompted them to run or they'd made a score so big that they could afford to disappear. Whatever it was, since Gavris was involved, she figured it happened out east.

For two weeks she collected data on crimes of all sorts for a period of six months before and a month after October 29th. She went to libraries, newspapers, town halls and police stations all around southwestern Connecticut and Westchester County, New York, where Gavris' Spotless Cleaners did their work. She gathered data on robberies, embezzlements, assaults, murders and anything else that she thought might be relevant. Then she identified the victims, the assailants, the companies they worked for and their addresses. Finally, she organized and summarized the data.

After having been out of contact with me for the better part of three weeks, one evening she simply knocked on the door of my house in Connecticut.

Jenny was visiting her sister in Boston again, so I answered. Maggie was standing there with thick legal briefcases in each hand and a big smile on her face.

"Maggie? What on earth are you doing here?"

I took the cases from her hands, put them on the ground and gave her a big hug.

She gave me a joking, nervous look and said, "You don't want to know."

After we caught up a bit, Maggie came clean. She explained she'd been in Greenwich and what she'd been doing. She ignored my admonishment and showed me her twelve-page list of crimes that had happened in my area in the months surrounding Emile and Bev and Stavros' disappearance. The summary had the name of the crime, the victim, the perpetrator and relevant addresses.

"Do any of these names or businesses mean anything to you?"

I went through the list again. "Not really. I've heard of a few of them, but I can't see how any are tied to Emile or Bev."

"Damn."

We sat staring at her list.

"Maybe something here would mean something to Michael Gavris, the son."

"What are you thinking?"

"That Gavris should see this list. To see if any of the names mean anything to him."

"I suppose I could show him."

"No, Phil. *We* should show him. I've put a ton of work into this and there isn't a snowball's hope in hell that I'm not going with you. And before you start to object, in addition to those two massive briefcases full of documents, I have more out in my rental car."

And to think that Jenny called me monomaniacal. I could learn from this woman.

Before I could mount any sort of objection, Maggie moved the conversation forward. "Do you think Michael Gavris is dishonest, the way his father was?"

I thought about it for a minute. "I'm not sure. I think he's pretty honest, but we're putting him in a terrible position."

"Why?"

"If we prove his father was a crook and it becomes public, he's going to lose a lot of business, maybe even go out of business."

"But we're looking into the disappearance of his own father. I don't care how strained their relationship was, he must want to know what happened."

"Unless he's a crook too."

"Exactly."

We sat there for a minute, both thinking.

"Aside from the fact that you did all of this work, and it is an amazing job, why do you have to be there?"

"What if he is a crook?"

"That's my point! He doesn't know you're involved or that you even exist. We should keep it that way."

"I understand what you're saying, but we can protect ourselves."

I burst out laughing at that. "You haven't met Michael Gavris. The guy is strong as an ox."

"I know."

"You know?"

"Sure. I've seen him. I've been doing research in this area for the sole purpose of approaching him for the better part of a month. Do you really think I wouldn't take a look to see what the guy looks like? Who he hangs around with?"

I started to respond, but she cut me off. "I was in a car. He never saw me."

I shook my head, frustrated by the risks she was taking. "Okay, so having seen him, how do you think you and I are going to protect ourselves against him?"

"We just tell him we've coordinated our efforts with your friend from the Greenwich PD."

"Mike Eastmure?"

"Yeah, with Mike."

"But why do you have to be there?"

"In case he's dirty."

"What do you mean?"

"You show him the list. Hold a piece of paper over it and go down, one name at a time. I'll watch his reaction to each name. If he's honest, great. If he's not, with two of us there, we at least have a chance of seeing names that register with him."

Chapter 38:

Gavris agreed to meet us the next afternoon at my office. I introduced Margaret as my assistant, trying to keep her part in it as minimal as I could. She went along.

As a result of Margaret's research, we had a list of many of his clients. She'd spent several days trailing Spotless Cleaner trucks and took note of the companies they visited. We added a few of his clients to the list, to test Gavris' honesty.

I told Gavris I really wanted him to think hard about each name I showed him, to think of any connection his father or Spotless might have with every single name. I made up some bullshit about how much easier it is to focus on individual names on a long list if you only look at one at a time. He agreed.

We started down the first page. Margaret buried a known client toward the bottom of the page as an early test.

When I exposed that name he paused and read the associated crime, burglary at a financial services firm, computers stolen. He acknowledged the company was a client.

We went through the two hundred and eighty-seven events on twelve pages over the course of forty minutes. Stavros never skipped a single planted client. More significantly, he identified eleven real events involving victims or criminals he thought his father knew. They included legitimate Spotless Cleaner clients, a dry cleaner, a dentist and some friends and acquaintances.

We questioned him about each of the eleven incidents and told him that we'd investigate each one and get back to him.

After he left, we examined Maggie's files on each of the eleven incidents. Five involved clients Spotless cleaned for and two of those were law firms. We spent a few days looking into all five. They could have been blackmailed or Stavros Gavris could have been stealing information from them, but we couldn't prove it. Four were still clients and the one who stopped using Spotless said they did it for economic reasons.

Next we looked at the dentist, a man named Mark Hayden in Katona, New York. Hayden was Stavros' dentist. His office had been robbed. The police report on the robbery was vague. When we asked Dr. Hayden about it, he said the whole thing was sort of odd. The thieves broke in late one night and forced open his drug cabinet. They only got away with small amounts of novocaine and nitrous oxide.

When we asked him about Stavros Gavris, Dr Hayden said he barely remembered him. He didn't know Gavris had gone missing. He'd thought that, like many patients, Gavris had simply changed dentists or moved away.

In spite of our efforts, we still had no idea what happened.

Chapter 39:

In the twenty years since I'd met Coulon I'd been suspected of murder, blackmail and extortion, held by the police in Ontario, questioned by the RCMP, the FBI, the Connecticut State Police and the Greenwich Police Department. I'd built a business, almost lost it and rebuilt it. I'd been threatened, pushed around and shot.

And I lost my wife of thirty years. Jenny told me she'd had enough and wanted a divorce.

Even though I sensed it was coming, the reality floored me. Losing Jenny was worse than getting shot. I spent the next few weeks operating in a fog.

She asked that I move out and I blindly, defeatedly agreed. I rented a small house in a middle-income beach community about thirty minutes east of New Canaan. It wasn't fancy, but it suited my depressed needs.

For the first time in almost forty years, I was alone. I hated it. I brooded and contemplated what I could do to get Jenny back. My discomfort with what I viewed as the tedium of our everyday existence had started a series of events that upended everything. I'd ruined the life she built for us and for herself. In the time since the initial upheaval, when I was suspected of murdering Emile and Bev, Jenny had tried to rebuild our lives and her own. Her life had changed, but she'd been able to move forward. I hadn't. I couldn't.

There was still a man out there who killed Emile and Bev and shot me. If it was Alversen, he'd gone quiet and was under such intense scrutiny that he no longer felt like much of a threat. That was good. If it wasn't Alversen I hadn't the faintest idea who it might be. That was bad. I wasn't getting anywhere.

Fortunately, Maggie was.

I told her about my separation and she left me alone for a month, giving me the space to get my new life in some order. In spite of all that had happened my business was doing well and almost running itself. I bought what I needed for my rental house and, once my doctors gave me the okay, started running again. For me running had always been therapeutic and between rehabbing from being shot and trying to cope with my separation, the exercise was a godsend.

I settled into a quiet, solitary, dark existence. I worked, ran and pursued every possible lead. Aside from occasional conversations with my sons, my interactions with other humans were minimal. I talked with clients, brokers, cashiers and food delivery people. I only engaged if I had to.

Then one afternoon there was a knock on my front door. Aside from food delivery people, no one ever visited me, especially unannounced. I'd given my address to Jenny and the boys, but I doubted any of them would surprise me on a weekday afternoon.

I opened the door and there, once again, was Maggie. She had a legal briefcase in one hand and a massive handbag in the other.

"What are you doing here? I thought you were in Chicago. How'd you get my new address?"

"How about 'Hi, Maggie. How are you?'"

"Well okay, hi. Come on in. Let me help you with your things."

As I hugged her and showed her in, I continued my questions.

"How did you find me?"

"Please."

"What are you doing here?"

"I found something, Phil."

"What?"

"I dug deeper into the events that Mike Gavris identified. I've spent the past few weeks revisiting each one."

Maggie looked around my house for the first time. The front hall was essentially empty and the living room had a couch, a chair, a coffee table and a tv.

"What have you been doing? This place needs some serious help."

"What did you find?"

"You remember the dentist whose office got broken into? Mark Hayden, Stavros' dentist?"

"Yeah."

"I went back to see him again. This time he wasn't as busy and gave Stavros' file a thorough look. He opened the file on his desk with me right there. As he was going through it, he noticed something odd."

"What?"

"He said that the x-rays he'd taken in recent years were in the folder, but the full baseline x-rays, the ones he takes the first time anyone comes into his office were missing."

"Missing?"

"Yeah. Gone."

"A physical file or computer files?"

"Physical."

"Does he still have computer records?"

Maggie smiled her infectious smile. "Yes. And a few physical older ones."

"Why would he keep the baselines in a folder? Why not keep everything on his computer?"

"Nowadays he does. He got a new system in 2014 but the old files didn't transfer well so he kept the old records. Gavris was an old client."

We walked into the kitchen and I got her a can of seltzer water. As I started to close the refrigerator door, she pulled it back open. Then she opened the freezer. The fridge was sparsely filled and, but for a few frozen dinners and ice, the freezer was empty. "What the hell, Phil? This is worse than the living room."

I ignored her. "What do you think that means? What's the significance of the missing baseline files?"

"I don't know, but Dr Hayden said the robbery was strange. He said it's rare that people break into dentists' offices to steal drugs. Why steal novocaine or lidocaine or nitrous oxide?"

"Are you saying the burglary was staged to steal Gavris' baseline dental records? Do we even know if that's when they went missing?"

"We don't know for sure. But what if it was?"

"Were other files missing?"

"None that Dr. Hayden is aware of."

"Maggie, why would anyone steal his file? You can't think..."

"How tall was Stavros Gavris?"

"I don't know. I haven't seen him in years."

"You know what I mean."

"Are you asking if he was short? Like Emile?"

"Was he?"

"Yes."

"How old was he when he disappeared?"

"I don't know."

"I do. He was sixty-eight."

"Hmm."

"Exactly."

"Emile was seventy-one."

"What are you saying? You think someone stole Gavris' dental records and somehow put them in Emile's dentist's files?"

Maggie nodded. "I think it's possible."

"But who would do that? Why would anyone do it?"

"There's only one person I can think of."

Chapter 40:

Rather than moving to a hotel, I talked Maggie into staying with me. My house had three bedrooms. I'd purchased beds and linens for all three rooms in case my kids wanted to stay with me. Maggie's reaction to the bedrooms wasn't any better than her reaction to the living room or the fridge.

"You're pathetic."

"You have everything you need, and there are towels and toiletries in the guest bathroom down the hall. Even toothpaste and stuff in the medicine cabinet."

She looked around one of the guest rooms, at the blank walls and into the empty closet. "Oh yeah. You thought of everything."

"What? There's a dresser, a nightstand, reading lights."

"Everything a girl needs."

"Shut up."

She laughed and grabbed her purse from the bed then headed for the front door.

"Where are you going?"

"Get your wallet. We're going shopping."

For the next few hours Maggie dragged me into what seemed like every furniture and home furnishing and electronics store within miles of my new home.

Chapter 41:

As we were driving, I called Detective Mike Eastmure of the Greenwich PD and asked him about Coulon's dental records. I had no idea who Emile's dentist was and even if I did know, I doubted the dentist would be willing to give me what I wanted. Eastmure said that during the initial investigation, after I had tentatively identified the bodies, it had been the state police who found Emile's dentist and gathered his records. He promised me he'd look into it.

Two days later Mike and Maggie and I were sitting in the office of Emile's dentist, a woman named Monika D'Agostino.

She explained that, as she had told the state police, Coulon had only visited her office once, for a cleaning. He had given her his old file, from a dentist in some other state. She'd wanted to do her own baseline x-rays, but Mr. Coulon had begged off, saying he'd been exposed to a lot of radiation from a car accident in the past two years and wanted to wait until she really needed them. It all sounded reasonable so she just put his old x-rays into her new file and had her technician clean his teeth.

Coulon's appointment had been on July 27th, 2012, three days after Hayden's office was robbed.

Dr. D'Agostino hadn't heard from him again.

Six and a half years later, the state police contacted her and asked if Emile Coulon had been her patient. She looked him up and found his file.

For the next two weeks I'd badgered Mike to get the state police to get an expert to compare the dental records Dr. D'Agostino had innocently provided as Coulon's with Stavros Gavris' more recent computer records at Dr. Hayden's office.

Eleven days later Mike Eastmure knocked on my front door. He was accompanied by Nancy Rhymer of the Connecticut State Police. Maggie answered the door.

"May I help you?"

I walked up behind her. Mike looked from Maggie to me and gave me a look.

I gave him a look back. Nothing was lost on Maggie. She rolled her eyes at Mike too.

He laughed and put up his hands, acknowledging his hasty misinterpretation.

I extended my hand to Rhymer and Mike, then introduced everyone. We led them into the kitchen, which was furnished with a new table and six chairs. I got everyone coffee.

"What's up? Do you have something?"

Mike smiled. "We do. You were right."

Maggie and I both asked, "The dental records were Gavris'?"

Eastmure looked to Connecticut State Police Officer Rhymer. She nodded and said, "Yes. We obtained copies of the dental files the FBI shared with the Ontario Provincial Police and our forensic dentists confirmed that the dental records matched those provided by Dr. Hayden."

I looked at Maggie. "Holy shit."

Rhymer continued. "The male body found on the island was that of Stavros Gavris. Not Emile Coulon."

Mike looked at me and said, "You were right."

I immediately corrected him. "Maggie was right. Because of her persistence Dr. Hayden discovered that Gavris' baseline images were missing from his files."

I turned back to Rhymer. "Were you able to re-confirm the identity of the female? Was it Bev?"

Rhymer nodded. "The two bodies are Stavros Gavris and Beverly Sutton."

"That motherfucker. He killed her."

Maggie nodded. "And he tried to kill you. It had to have been him."

Chapter 42:

A few days later, Emile Coulon's picture was everywhere. He was a person of interest in two murders, one attempted murder and an extensive, multi-state extortion scheme. The nature of his crimes caught the public's interest, and the story went viral.

Once again, my life became a living hell. The media was camped outside my door. True-crime shows were pleading with me to talk with them. I flatly refused.

Fortunately, Maggie and I anticipated the media storm and she moved back to Chicago before the deluge. That helped, but only a little. Several reporters questioned my new neighbors and discovered that a woman had been staying with me periodically. One reporter and her network assumed the seediest and ran with it. Others quickly followed suit.

While the media's misinterpretation of my relationship with Maggie led to some complicated conversations with Jenny and my children, other aspects of their reporting were beneficial. I was no longer a suspect in the murders. That made the rest of my family's lives a lot easier.

I was glad to be in the clear with the police too, but angrier than ever. I had believed that Emile was my friend. More importantly, Bev had considered him her closest friend and her lover. She had devoted her life to him and he killed her.

With his face plastered everywhere, I felt sure he'd be found, and quickly. But days passed and then weeks. So far as I knew, he was gone.

Chapter 43:

Three months later there was still no sign of Emile. The media's interest dwindled and, so far as I could tell, the police's had too. The lack of progress was increasingly frustrating.

While managing my fund was financially rewarding, except on the most volatile of days, it wasn't exactly exciting. And whatever thrill I'd gotten from snooping around in other people's lives and uncovering their indiscretions seemed trivial. From the day I drove back to Canada and turned myself into the authorities, my life changed. Trying to convince them that I wasn't a murderer or to convince Hendrie that I wasn't a blackmailer had been terrifying, but also wildly challenging, even thrilling. The adrenaline rush of matching wits with them and of trying to bring down Alversen made everyday life mundane.

When I'd worked for Emile, I thought I'd been feeding some dark side of my nature. Some of the relatively innocent people I'd investigated had been hurt and a person I thought was a friend had been murdered, another was a murderer. I learned I wasn't dark; I'd just been bored. Now I wanted to set things right. And the challenge of doing that, the stakes involved, were unlike anything I'd ever experienced before.

I'd been desperate for my life to return to normal. And now that it had, I was beyond restless.

My sense was that Maggie felt the same way. She had a high-powered job that taxed her mind, but she needed more.

She found excuses to come stay with me. And her company was welcome.

One night as we were making dinner from my newly stocked pantry, Maggie asked me why I thought Emile killed Bev and Stavros. We'd speculated that maybe he'd made a huge score, but that didn't explain why he felt compelled to kill his partners.

"Maybe he was tired of dividing the take."

Maggie looked at me. "That could possibly explain killing Gavris, but why Bev? Why would he kill his partner of all those years? His lover?"

"I don't know. Maybe when he killed Gavris, Bev freaked out and he killed her too."

"How could he kill someone he loved?"

"Loved?"

"Don't you think he loved her?"

I thought about that for a minute as I rinsed the kale or spinach or whatever it was she had me cleaning.

"I don't know. Clearly, I didn't really know Emile. The guy lied to me every day. He extorted money and he killed two people."

"But do you think he loved her?"

"I don't know. I think he was – is – a sociopath. Are sociopaths capable of loving?"

I looked from the sink to Maggie. She was crying.

I took her in my arms and held her. I didn't know why she was crying, but I suspect it was because she felt so alone. I held her tight.

I wanted to kiss her but didn't. If I was ever going to kiss Maggie, I had to mean it. And while I was strongly drawn to her and did want to comfort her, after a nearly forty-year relationship with Jenny, I wasn't ready to give up. I still loved her. Maggie deserved much more than I could give.

Chapter 44:

The next morning when I walked into the kitchen, she was sitting at the table drinking a cup of coffee.

"Where do you think he is?"

I burst out laughing.

"What?"

I kept laughing and she started to laugh too.

She said, "Do you need a post-non-coital pep talk?"

I laughed harder.

She smiled her smile and said, "Shut up."

"You alright?"

She looked at me. I could tell I'd hurt her but I hoped she knew why.

I sat and reached across the table, taking her hand.

"I've been with Jenny for almost forty years, since college. You're still young and I'm a long way from that."

"Stop, Phil. I get it."

I squeezed her hand.

She rolled her eyes.

"What, Maggie?"

"Seriously, where would he go?"

I knew she was intentionally changing the subject, for both our sakes. "You're relentless."

She gave me a heartbreaking look that said she had to be.

"If he had all the money he ever needed, what would he do with it?"

And with that, a bell rang.

"Holy shit."

"What?"

"I think I know how we can find him."

Three minutes later we were on my laptop, looking at the Boston Whaler website.

"Are you telling me that with all the money he could ever need, you think he would want to buy a little outboard?"

Ignoring her, I scrolled through the website.

"This is a Boston Whaler 420 Outrage."

We looked at a few pictures of a beautiful forty-three-foot center console fishing boat. I scrolled down to the asking price: $950,000.

"A million bucks for a Whaler?"

I nodded and explained how much Emile loved to fish and that I remembered him ogling a decked-out Whaler up near Bar Harbor, Maine, back in the late '90s.

"Twenty years ago?"

"I know. But I can't tell you how many times he talked about big, tricked-out center console fishing boats. He told me that if he ever got rich, the first thing he'd buy was a top-of-the-line Boston Whaler Outrage."

"So what? We look at high-end Whaler sales?"

"We can sort it down a little finer than that, but essentially, yes, that's what I'm saying."

"Where?"

"On the water."

She gave me her 'duh' look.

"He's a bit of a xenophobe."

"So a racist, blackmailing, murderer. Lovely friend."

I ignored her. "And after spending most of his adult life in Connecticut and sometimes in Chicago, I'm pretty sure he'd base himself somewhere warm. He hated being cold."

"Okay. We've narrowed it down to the southern United States."

"As smart as he is, I doubt he'd buy it anywhere near where he planned to live. But still, if we can find out where he bought it, if he bought one, then we'll have the beginnings of a trail."

Chapter 45:

That same morning, I contacted Nancy Rhymer of the Connecticut State Police. She connected me with Tim Wright, the FBI agent in charge of investigating Coulon.

Wright was a smart, results-oriented man and he was as frustrated with the case as Maggie and I were. While he felt checking high-end Whaler sales was a stretch, he admitted he didn't have any better ideas. He told us he'd look into it.

From my perspective, there were few phrases that were more frustrating than 'I'll look into it'. Wright had no obligation to me and, if anything, he was probably prohibited from sharing anything he did find. I doubted I'd hear back from him.

Neither Maggie nor I found that acceptable. Thankfully her background gave her access to resources that mine did not. She sometimes researched consumer or voter reaction to various products or ideas. While she didn't have any experience researching high-end consumer luxury products, she knew a guy who knew a guy.

As Maggie worked it from the top down, I went at it from the bottom up. The nearest Boston Whaler dealership was Lark Marina in Norwalk, Connecticut.

I drove to Norwalk and walked into the Lark showroom. It was a quiet Tuesday morning and I was the only person, customer or salesperson, on the floor. There were about a dozen boats on display, a combination of Whalers and SeaRays. I looked at a mid-sized, mid-priced Whaler and worked my way up. After a few minutes, I heard footsteps from somewhere above me, where a row of offices overlooked two sides of the showroom.

"Can I help you?"

I looked up around, trying to find the source of the voice. "Over here."

A man who looked to be my age was walking along the left side of an open second floor hallway, toward the steps.

"Hi. Yes, please."

"I'll be right down."

As he made his way down the steps, I walked toward him.

"Hi. I'm Ward Chapdelaine."

"Phil Osgood."

"Are you interested in an Outrage?"

I paused. "Actually, I'm not."

"A SeaRay?"

"No."

He gave me a quizzical look.

"Do you have a minute?"

He looked around the empty showroom and shrugged his shoulders.

"Sure. What's up?"

"I'm trying to track someone down. Someone who I think bought a loaded Outrage."

Ward shrugged again, but this time turned his hands and palms upward.

"I can't give out information like that."

"I understand, but if I explain the circumstances, maybe you could help me?"

That quizzical look again.

"I'm trying to track down a murderer."

"Are you a cop?"

"No. I sometimes work as a private investigator."

"Sometimes? Are you licensed?"

"No."

"I really don't see how I can help you."

He looked like he was about done with me.

"The guy I'm looking for killed a friend of mine and another guy. It happened eight years ago. I'm still trying to find the bastard."

His next words caught me by surprise.

"Are you looking for Emile Coulon?"

I thought, 'Fuck, I've blown it.' But I nodded. "You know him?"

"Yeah, everyone around here knew Emile. We all liked him."

"So did I."

"How did you know him?"

"Did you read about the case? Back when the bodies were found up in Canada?"

"Yeah."

"Well, I'm the idiot he framed for the murders." I paused and then added, "And shot."

Ward shook his head. "Holy shit."

"Holy shit is right."

"How do you think I can help you?"

I looked around the open showroom.

"Let's go up to my office."

Once we settled into his office, I simply told him the truth.

"No one has seen him since 2012. He could be hiding anywhere. The FBI and the police in Ontario and Connecticut tried to find him, but they're not making any progress."

"So why do you think you can find him?"

"I don't know if I can, but I have to try."

He didn't react.

"He killed Bev. She was loyal to him for over twenty years. It's one thing to use me and to blackmail a bunch of rich guys, but Bev devoted her life to him. She loved him. And the son-of-a-bitch killed her."

Chapdelaine seemed to reach a decision. "So how can I help you?"

I smiled gratefully and calmed down.

"First of all, how did you know Emile?"

"He rented boats from us sometimes, part of our 'Captain's Program'."

"And you remember him from that?"

"The guy had the gift of gab. We've got some pretty good salespeople around here and he charmed all of us."

"Believe me, I get it."

We both chuckled, but Chapdelaine got serious. "I never figured him as a murderer. I knew he was slick, but I would have never thought he could do all the shit he's done."

"From what I understand, your outfit, Lark Marine, is affiliated with Marine Max. And they're the biggest seller of Whaler's in the country."

"Yeah."

"Emile and I spent some time together on boats, fishing and for work. He always said that if he had all the money in the world, he'd get himself a thirty-eight-foot Boston Whaler Outrage with three or four Mercury engines and a flying bridge and rig the thing with every toy known to man."

"And since he was blackmailing all these rich people..."

"He has all the money he could ever want."

"And you think he bought the boat."

"After all these years, it's the best idea I've got."

"Did you tell the Feds about it?"

"Yeah. They listened, but I don't think they bought it. I think it struck them as a wild goose chase."

He gave me a look. "It might be." He thought about it for a minute. "What you're doing isn't going to work."

I stifled a stab of disappointment and asked, "Why?"

He smiled, a great ball-buster's smile. He would have liked Bev. "Because you're going about it all wrong."

"What do you mean?"

"Marine Max is the biggest seller of Whalers in the country, but they still only sell about 40%. There's a better than fifty-fifty chance he bought it somewhere else. You could do all this work and come up empty."

"If he even bought a boat."

"If he even bought one."

I sensed he was holding back.

"Do you have a better idea?"

He smiled another smile, one that I suspected had sold a lot of boats. "I do."

Laughing I said, "Come on. You're killing me."

"Even if you could get into Marine Max's corporate records, you'd only have a 50% chance of finding Emile's hypothetical boat."

"Right."

"But, what does every person who buys a Whaler get?"

I tried to figure it out, but shrugged.

"A warranty."

"Holy shit."

Ward smiled from ear to ear. "And Boston Whaler, who is owned by Brunswick, provides that warranty. So they would have a list of every Whaler sold from 2012 until today, with information about the buyer."

I was literally giddy with excitement.

"That is down-right brilliant. Honestly, in twenty minutes you've come up with a better idea than I've had in two years."

Ward laughed. "We're here to help."

We basked for a moment in the glory of a really good idea.

"I guess your next step'll be to go back to the FBI and ask them to get a warrant." He gave an easy laugh. "It's either that or hack into Brunswick's Boston Whaler warranty database."

I chuckled too. I doubted FBI Agent Wright or his bosses would sanction the man hours to investigate every owner for a longshot on an eight-year-old Canadian murder case.

Chapter 46:

Two days later as I was finishing a lunchtime run, I found Maggie standing in my driveway, waiting for me.

Inside, she sat at the kitchen table as I poured two glasses of iced tea.

"Come on, Maggie. What's going on?"

I handed her an iced tea and sat at my normal seat.

"Your friend Chapdelaine was right."

I gave her an exasperated look. "I know he was right, but I seriously doubt the FBI is going to commit the resources they need to research every possible warranty."

"We don't need them." She paused, baiting me.

"He gave you two suggestions. Go to the Feds or..."

"Or crack Boston Whaler's database."

Maggie took a long sip of her tea. I waited, letting her tease me. Finally, she looked at me and smiled.

"I know a guy."

I stared at her for a minute and, for about the twentieth time, asked, "Who do you work for?"

Chapter 47:

Four days later we were back at the kitchen table, this time sitting side-by-side, looking at Brunswick's internal website. Maggie had clearly already spent some time figuring out how to navigate the site. She clicked into the warranty section and refined her search from there. She had access to warranties on every Boston Whaler Outrage sold since 2007. We decided to back-check in case he bought a used one.

I looked from the screen to her in amazed awe.

She opened a file and then a sub file and then another. The name of an owner, his address, the marina who sold the boat and the boat's specific options popped up.

"Wow."

She smiled. "It's exactly what we need."

She reached to type something else into the computer and I took her hand and pulled it back.

"What?"

"We're breaking the law."

Maggie was as honest as I was and, in spite of my ignorance about what she actually did for a living, I knew she didn't take breaking the law lightly.

"We're catching a murderer."

We looked at each other and reached a tacit agreement.

For the next few we days gathered information on every Boston Whaler Outrage sold since '07 from Maine to Florida to Texas and along the Pacific coast from California to Washington. There were thousands of sales.

We parsed the list.

From what I could remember, Emile's dream boat was at least thirty-eight feet long, had three Mercury outboard engines and a flying bridge. There were almost seven-hundred sales of Outrages matching that criteria, sold through seventy-three different dealers.

We sorted the sales by region and date. Then we started investigating.

The warranty documents included names and addresses, emails and sometimes even phone numbers. Some of the names were corporations or LLCs, but there was always at least an address and contact information. Emile wouldn't be using his real name – if he did he'd be in jail, but whatever alias he was using might be on our list.

The warranty transferred with sales and could often be extended, so even if he bought a used boat, his Outrage was probably on our list. If he bought one.

There still were too many names. Seven hundred was too many. But seventy-three was not. We decided to visit the dealers.

Chapter 48:

Our first stop was in Maine.

The northern most east coast dealer on our list was in Rockland, Maine. One of the six hundred and ninety-two Outrages on our list had been sold there.

After lengthy discussion and some truly hair-brained schemes, we decided to do what we usually did and go with the truth. But since we were lawbreakers, we couldn't tell the whole truth – that we had hacked the Boston Whaler warranty database. We decided to just ask if they had sold any Outrages matching our description.

The Rockland dealership turned out to be a good starting point. A kid in the showroom pointed us in the direction of the boatyard's owner, Mark Masselink, who was sitting out by the water, talking on his cellphone.

Even on the phone he had a loud voice and booming laugh people in Bar Harbor might hear. When he saw us coming, he ended his call and stood to greet us. He was a big guy, maybe 6'3" with a bigger smile and a welcoming personality. He was wearing beat-up cargo shorts, a bright lime-green silky short-sleeved shirt, a goofy hat, two pairs of glasses hanging around his neck and work boots that could only be described as pleather.

We introduced ourselves and I got to the point. "We have sort of an odd question for you."

Masselink laughed his loud laugh. "My favorite kind."

"Do you remember selling a Boston Whaler Outrage, between thirty-eight and forty-three feet, with three Mercury outboards and a flying bridge? I think it would have been sometime between 2012 and 2015."

He gave another laugh. Then, "Can I ask why you want to know?"

I told him the short version of the truth, that we suspected a murderer named Emile Coulon had purchased one.

"You think he bought it here?"

"To be honest I don't know."

He thought about that for a moment then asked, "What's your plan? Are you going to visit every Whaler dealership in the country?" He sounded incredulous.

We both nodded.

Aware of his geography he smiled and said, "Please tell me I'm last and not first?"

Maggie held up a single finger.

He looked at us like we were crazy, then sympathetically.

"I'm sorry. I did sell a boat like that, but I know the owner." He pointed to a picture we had of Coulon. "It wasn't him."

"You're sure?"

"Yup. A man name Gordon Clapp owns the one I sold."

"Coulon is probably using an alias."

Masselink laughed. "I'm pretty sure this guy isn't Coulon. Gordon's my father-in-law."

Chapter 49:

It wasn't always as easy as Rockland. Sometimes the marina owner had changed or the broker who dealt with the client who bought an Outrage had moved on, so no one remembered the buyer's face, but with a little legwork we were able to cross off sixteen boats and six dealers.

When we got home, Maggie told me she had to go to Chicago for a while, for work. I was afraid there was more to it. For over a month, we'd been spending at least a few days a week living together and, while we had never so much as kissed, there was a tension building, one that neither of us was comfortable with. A little time apart seemed like a good idea.

I worked my way down the east coast, stopping at every Whaler dealer on our list. When I could, if the dealers knew where boats meeting our criteria that they sold were located, I visited the actual boat and set eyes on its owner. When that wasn't possible, I walked around the boatyard where the Outrage was normally docked or serviced and showed the people who worked there Emile's picture.

By the time I reached Florida, I'd visited twenty-eight dealers and tentatively eliminated two hundred and seventy-three of the boats on our list. Along the way there had been seven boats that the original dealer had lost track of. I gave Maggie the details on those. She traced their ownership and warranty records. Rather than physically backtracking she emailed photos of Emile to boat brokers involved in the sales and marinas where the boats were serviced. Her luck was no better than mine.

Five days into the Florida leg, Maggie met me in West Palm Beach. We updated each other on our findings and quickly fell back into our old routine. I was amazed by how much I'd missed her but was careful to hide my feelings. I was still talking regularly, even frequently with Jenny. I missed her too, in a different way and more. I wanted Jenny back in my life, I needed her. It wasn't clear how she felt.

Maggie traveled with me for a few days, then headed back to Chicago. Two days later, I picked her up at the airport in Sarasota. Over the eight weeks since we'd started in Maine, we'd visited forty-one marinas.

Her flight was two hours late so by the time she was in my car, it was past 3pm. We almost decided to call it a day and find a hotel, but the Sarasota Marine Max had four boats on our list.

It was a big operation and unlike many of the sleepy marinas we'd visited, Sarasota's actually had a receptionist. When we explained why we were there she said the marina had changed ownership in 2017, but several of the brokers had been around for over a decade. She took us to the office of a veteran broker named Jane McDonald.

After we were seated in her small office, we told Jane what we were up to. Like many of the people we dealt with, she seemed sympathetic and genuinely interested in helping.

As I was describing the specifics of Coulon's dream Outrage, McDonald interrupted. "Why don't you just show me the guy's picture. I'll either recognize him or I won't."

We smiled and showed her the picture. We were so used to getting a quick 'no' that McDonald's response caught us by surprise.

"I know this guy. He did buy an Outrage here."

Maggie and I both gasped. "You do? He did?"

"Yeah. He had hair and a beard, but I recognize his blue eyes and his smile."

"Are you sure?"

"Absolutely. His name wasn't Coulon though."

Jane looked from the photo to her computer. We had four

names on our list, but we both waited quietly as she typed away.

"Here it is. A thirty-eight-foot Outrage, sold in November of 2012. Custom ordered."

We waited for the name.

"Sold to, let's see, to Martin Emmett."

It was the second name on our list.

We could barely contain our excitement. Maggie spoke first. "Are you sure?"

McDonald typed for a few more seconds and said "Yes, positive. I just couldn't remember his name."

I wanted to be sure. "What do you remember about him?"

"He was funny as hell. Great guy." She caught herself. "Are you sure he's a murderer?"

Maggie and I both nodded. Maggie asked, "Anything else? Was he with anyone?"

"No. He was always alone when I saw him."

"Was he here many times?"

"Not at first. When you custom order a boat like his, loaded, it takes months to get it. We met when he ordered it, just a few times, if I remember correctly."

"Is that unusual?"

"Unusual yes, but it happens. Some guys who buy boats like this know every detail of what they want. They've often thought about it for years. Your guy was like that."

I gave Maggie a satisfied look.

"You said he wasn't here much – at first. What did you mean?"

"Boston Whaler builds the boats over in Edgewater, but a lot of the extras are added here. Marty had a ton of extras on his boat. I think we worked on it for a couple of weeks after it was delivered. He visited us a few times to place the order, then left. But once the boat was delivered here, he hung around while we worked on it. I think he was staying at a motel nearby."

We spent the next twenty minutes discussing details with McDonald. For the paperwork associated with the purchase, Emile gave an address in Panama City, Florida. But for the boat's registration with the state of Florida, he gave her a different address, a PO box in Panama City.

Maggie asked, "Does the registration take time? Is it something they would have mailed to him?"

McDonald nodded. "The first year we'd have done all the paperwork for him. After that every year the DMV would send him a renewal form or he could pick one up at any branch in the state. Once he filled out the form and paid, they'd mail him updated registration papers and the stickers for his bow, usually a few weeks later."

"So if he moved, could he just go to a DMV and get new forms and give them a new address?"

"Yup."

Maggie and I shared a disappointed glance.

Jane said she knew someone else who might be able to help. She walked us over to the marina's extensive boat-works area and introduced us to an elderly mechanic named Greg Henderson. Jane remembered that he and Emile had become friends.

She introduced us and then showed Greg our picture of Emile. "Do you remember this guy?"

The second Henderson saw the picture, a smile came across his weathered face. "Sure. That's Marty Emmett. The little wise ass. I'll never forget him."

Jane laughed. "You don't know the half of it."

Henderson studied the picture and started to laugh. "I told you it was a toupee."

Jane laughed again. "You did."

"What's up? Why are you asking about Marty?"

Maggie spoke up. "Did you know him well?"

"Not really. But while he was here, while we were working on his boat, we sometimes had dinner together or beers over at Annie's."

McDonald interjected, "Annie's is a bar a few blocks away."

"Did he ever tell you where he was going? Where he planned on keeping the boat?"

"Yeah. I think he said he had moved to Panama City, on the panhandle. He was going to keep it there. Why are you looking for him?"

Jane jumped in. "They think he murdered two people, up in Canada."

Chapter 50:

Thirty seconds after I stepped into my hotel room, Maggie knocked on my door. For about the fifth time since we'd left the marina, she said, "I can't believe we found him. I mean, we haven't exactly found him but we're on his trail. You were right, Phil. He bought the boat."

We looked at each other, both still in shock. "I was so used to getting no for an answer that when Jane said yes, I almost didn't hear it."

"Me neither."

"I guess our next step is to call Tim Wright at the FBI."

A look of disappointment crossed Maggie's face, one I shared. She said, "I suppose we have to."

"I don't want to either. I want to drive to Panama City and find the bastard on our own. But we can't. We have to call."

"Before we do, let's do a little more research."

"What research?"

"First, let's check the warranty file on his boat again."

I looked Maggie straight in the eyes, but she pretended not to see and instead pulled out her laptop, logged into the motel's Wifi and into the Brunswick site, then pulled up Martin Emmett's warranty information.

"He ordered the boat in July of 2012 and picked it up in November, right after he killed them. He must have planned the whole thing out. For months."

"How cold could the bastard possibly be?"

She shook her head. "Do you think Bev knew about the boat?"

"If he was planning on killing her, I doubt it. I doubt he'd have given her information she might inadvertently share."

"Since he knew he was going to have to go into hiding."

"Exactly."

I still couldn't believe how cold-hearted he was. I tried not to imagine Bev's last moments, how betrayed she must have felt, how scared.

Maggie stayed focused. "He bought the boat in 2012, so the component warranty has expired, it only lasts three years. But the hull warranty is ten years. His boat's still covered."

"What address did he use for the warranty?"

"Panama City. The same one he gave to Jane."

She opened a fresh page and googled the address. Then she zoomed in on a modest one-story house.

Chapter 51:

My call to Special Agent Tim Wright of the FBI was made more interesting by the fact that I didn't tell him the whole truth. I told him that two people at the Marine Max Marina in Sarasota identified Emile Coulon as the man who purchased a Boston Whaler Outrage in November of 2012 using the alias Martin Emmett. I also gave him Emmett's Panama City address.

When Wright asked how I made the discovery I explained that my associate and I had traveled from Maine to Florida, stopping at almost every marina that sold Boston Whaler's and that at each marina we showed pictures of Coulon and Sutton to anyone who would look.

I didn't tell him that I had a list of every sale since 2007.

Wright found my explanation dubious. I encouraged him to call each of the other forty marinas I'd visited to verify my story. He didn't take me up on that offer, but did ask that I provide him with the names of the two people at Marine Max in Sarasota.

As we finished our call Agent Wright once again told me he'd get back to me. I smiled a satisfied smile. This time I knew he would.

After he rang off, Maggie and I debated calling my contacts at the Connecticut State Police and at the Ontario Provincial Police to give them the information as well. We wanted to put as much pressure on the FBI as we could, but we didn't want to do anything to spook Coulon. He didn't know we knew he'd purchased an Outrage or that he was using the alias Martin Emmett.

Chapter 52:

The next morning when we started our seven-hour drive to Panama City, Maggie was as excited as I was. "Do you think he's going to be there?"

"No. He's too smart for that. But for the first time, I think we might actually catch him."

"I wish I believed that, Phil."

"We've set the Feds up to succeed. They can find him so many ways now. Even if he is using another alias, so long as he's using his boat we can get him."

"How?"

"First, we know his boat's make and model and the registration numbers. The Feds will spread the word and within a day or two every marina, gas pump and floating cop in the country will be looking for Emile's Outrage."

Maggie nodded. "That's good. And?"

"And he has to re-register the boat every year."

"Yeah, but we'll only know that after the fact. And when I say "we" I mean the FBI, not us."

"They have the boat's VIN. All they have to do is flag it. When he updates his registration, it'll set off alarms at the DMV he chooses and bingo."

"And he has to give the DMV an address. A place to mail the registration and bow stickers."

"Exactly. So even if they don't catch him at the DMV or he registers online –"

"He has to give them an address, somewhere he can pick up the papers and bow stickers."

"So the Feds will have plenty of time to set up surveillance to catch him when he picks up his new registration – weeks later."

Maggie gave me a frustrated look.

"What?"

"He bought it in November of 2012. If he's still on that same cycle, he won't be renewing it again until next November. We'll have to wait for five months."

"It's worse than that. Florida registrations all renew in February."

Seven hours later we approached the house Emile had given as his address in Panama City: 1467 Delmar Road. The house was modest, not more than five or six rooms and in desperate need of a paint job. A young mother was sitting in front of the house, on a plastic lawn chair, reading as two little kids played in the dried-out, dirt covered front yard.

"This doesn't look like a place where a guy with a million-dollar boat would live."

"I doubt he ever lived here. He didn't finance the boat, so it's not likely that the people at the Marine Max in Sarasota checked his address or any of the information he gave them. They got their cashier's check."

"I wonder if the FBI or the police have been here yet."

As we drove past, we both scanned the cars parked along the road, looking for officers or agents who might be watching the house. We didn't see anyone.

Our next stop was the town hall. There was no record of Coulon having lived at 1467 Delmar.

Following our last lead, we headed to the spot Emile had listed as his home marina. Another bust.

We'd have to wait the eight months.

Chapter 53:

I drove back home to Connecticut and Maggie flew back to Chicago.

This time Agent Wright of the FBI was actually grateful for the lead we'd given him and did become more forthcoming. He told me that every year since 2013, Coulon had paid for the next year's registration at a different DMV in different parts of Florida. Last November he'd done it at a DMV in Fort Lauderdale, on the east coast. He had the registration papers and boat stickers sent to a rented mailbox at a UPS store in nearby Pompano. The UPS store had video surveillance, but only kept recordings for the prior thirty days. They did have a record of a Martin Emmett renting the mailbox for three months, but that didn't do us any good.

So we waited. By late August I was climbing the walls. Then Maggie called me.

"He sold the boat."

"What?"

"He sold it. To a guy named Harrison Pool."

"How do you know? When did it happen?"

"He sold it six months ago in Seabrook, Texas, just outside of Houston."

"Shit."

"That's only the half of it. You're not going to believe the timing."

"What do you mean?"

"He sold it on December 4th, a day or two before we went to the police with the idea that Emile's dental records had been swapped."

"Before we told anyone?"

In an instant I reached the same conclusion Maggie must have.

"Shit. He's been watching me. God, Maggie. He must know about you."

She was quiet on the other end of the phone. "Maybe it wasn't him. He could have hired a private investigator."

"You might be right. It would be awfully risky for him to be here, where so many people know him. But that's not what matters right now. You can't be alone for another minute. You need to get out here right away. Are you in Chicago or DC?"

"DC."

"Come back to Connecticut. You can work from my place and we can work on catching him together. It's just too risky for you to stay alone."

"Okay."

"Wait. Do you know anyone there? Can you get someone to stay with you right now? Someone safe? From work or something?"

"Do you really think I need to?"

"Please, do that first. Call someone you trust and get them there now. Please, Maggie. And stay with them until you're on the plane or the train."

"Okay."

Four hours later she was on a train. I met her later that night at the station. I hugged her tight.

"I don't think I've ever been happier to see anyone."

She smiled.

"I'm so sorry I've gotten you into this mess."

"I got myself into this mess, Phil. You tried to keep me out of it."

I took her bags, looked nervously around and hurried her to my car. As we drove back to my house in Fairfield, Maggie looked worried.

"He sold the boat before we met with the police. Do you know what that means?"

I thought about it for a moment. When Maggie first researched crimes in the Connecticut area, I didn't even know she was here.

"Shit. He was following you, not me."

Maggie just nodded.

My mind leaped around the calendar. "It means he must have followed you here from Chicago. The first time you came to my house was after you finished the research."

"Not exactly."

"What do you mean?"

"I came here once, two weeks into that trip. I was going to tell you what I was up to."

"Why didn't you come in?"

"Jenny was here. I didn't want to interrupt you guys."

I thought back. Jenny had come to my rental house a few times in my first month there to bring me some stuff and to discuss our situation.

"Could anyone have seen you? Did you get out of your car?"

"Yes. I parked on the street and was walking toward your driveway when I saw you and Jenny in the window. I turned around and …"

I watched her face. She realized something.

"What?"

"It couldn't have been a private eye, they wouldn't have recognized me or followed me. It must have been him."

I caught up with her thought process. "It's hard to believe he could have hired a PI anyway. Emile's a known murderer. Even the dumbest investigator or closest friend would worry that he was just helping set up another attempt on my life."

She looked me straight in the eyes. "So he was watching you."

"And when he saw you, the day you came to my driveway, he started following you."

We both looked out the front window of my living room, out over the road.

"When did you visit the dentist whose office Emile stole Gavris dental records from?"

"Dr. Hayden."

"Yeah, Hayden."

She thought for a bit then said, "A few days after I saw Jenny at your place. I came back the second time right after I saw Hayden. When he discovered that Gavris' dental records were missing I had to tell you. I came straight from his office."

We looked at a calendar. Maggie checked her notes. The first time Maggie had visited him, before we met with Michael Gavris, Hayden hadn't had much time. He hadn't noticed that some of the dental images in Stavros Gavris' file were missing. He discovered they were gone on her second visit.

"If he was following you from your aborted visit, when you saw Jenny here, once he saw you at Hayden's office he must have known you'd discovered the missing records."

"And from there he must have realized we were going to put it all together."

"So he hurried back to Houston, to sell the boat."

"Do you really think that would be enough for him to sell it? What would make him think we even knew about it?"

"I don't know. Maybe he figured even if we didn't know about it, once it was known he was alive his picture would be everywhere."

"And it would be very difficult to sell the boat without being recognized."

"For sure. Even used, it must have been worth a half a million bucks. He'd have wanted to unload it while he still could, before everyone knew him."

"I guess."

"I think we should go there."

She looked surprised. "To Texas? Do you think that's a good idea? Won't that be dangerous?"

"He won't be there. The place will be crawling with cops and Feds."

We were quiet for a minute then Maggie said, "I'm surprised he didn't come after us. Try to kill us both."

"Maybe he was afraid to. He tried to kill me and failed. Because you saved me."

I regretted the words as soon as they came out of my mouth.

"And he saw the same papers everyone else did. He knew I helped save you."

"He must have."

"Jesus. I'm surprised he didn't try to come after me when he saw me come out of Hayden's office. At that point you didn't know about the missing records. You didn't even know I was back in Connecticut."

Chapter 54:

The next day we flew to Houston and drove down to Seabrook, to the marina where Emile's boat was docked. The place was crawling with FBI agents and police officers. Special Agent Wright was among them. He didn't look happy to see us.

He walked up to the cordoned-off entry to the dock and told the officer there to let us through. We ducked under the crime scene tape.

"What are you doing here? How could you possibly know he sold the boat?"

I took the question as rhetorical and shrugged.

Wright gave us a hard stare but led us down the dock. Emile's Whaler was near the end.

The three of us stood looking at the boat. It was called 'Reconnoiter.'

To his credit, Wright turned to Maggie and me and said, "When you told me you thought that Coulon might have purchased a Boston Whaler Outrage and that we might be able to track it down and find him as a result, I thought you were nuts."

We both smiled.

"And when I told my bosses that I thought it was worth looking into, they thought I was absolutely nuts."

I looked him straight in the eyes. "Did you look?"

He smiled back at us but didn't respond. They hadn't.

Before Maggie and I could share more than a satisfied glance our attention was drawn to a man hurrying down the dock toward us. Agent Wright introduced us to Harrison Poole, the man who bought Emile's boat. Wright didn't explain who we were.

"Mr. Poole and I spoke earlier. I showed him our file pictures and he confirmed that it was Coulon who sold him the boat."

Poole nervously interjected, "He wasn't bald and he had a beard, but it was him. He said his name was Martin Emmett. I assumed he was telling the truth. I had no idea about any of this."

The poor man was clearly a wreck. He'd spent a fortune on the boat and wasn't sure what was going to happen.

I was in no position to question Poole, so I asked Wright directly, "Were you able to trace Mr. Poole's payment?"

"We can discuss that later."

We looked back at the boat. An FBI forensics team was going over every inch of it.

Wright tapped me on the elbow, turning me back up the dock. "There's nothing we can do here. We've set up an office up in the marina. Come on."

Wright shook Poole's hand and started back up the dock. Maggie and I took another look at the Whaler. We'd spent months trying to find the boat and had barely glimpsed at it.

Chapter 55:

The marina's main building was under construction. When Wright finished with Poole he led us past the construction site, to a nearby trailer.

"There was a fire here. Half of the old marina building burned down."

"That's too bad."

"It burned down last December, on the 4th."

"The day he sold the boat?"

"That night."

"You think it was Coulon?"

"It would be a hell of a coincidence if it wasn't." Wright went on. "They closed on the boat late that afternoon. Poole confirmed it."

"So why the fire?"

"The paperwork on the sale. It was all burned. Poole said the boat broker had all the paperwork, that he was going to make copies and file the sale the next day."

I asked, "Is that why we only just learned about the sale?"

Wright nodded. "I guess so. I'll track down the broker and get more details. But the marina's owner said everything was backed up for months after the fire. They only started filing old paperwork a few weeks ago."

"How'd you discover the sale?"

"We had the boat's VIN flagged. When the sale finally went through the system we were notified." Wright turned to face Maggie. "The more interesting question remains, how do you two know about the sale?" There was an uncomfortable silence. As Maggie fumbled a response, Wright held up his hands. "Never mind. I don't want to know."

Over the next few weeks the Feds gathered as much information as they could on the money trail surrounding the sale. Wright shared some of the information with us.

Poole had paid Emile with a cashier's check made out to Martin Emmett. Emmett deposited it into his checking account at a regional bank, Loan Star Trust, and promptly had that money and the rest of the money in the account wired to an account in Switzerland. The Loan Star account was closed two days after the transfer went through.

The Feds were able to find video footage of the *Reconnoiter* being gassed up at the marina prior to the sale. The man in the video was built like Coulon, but he was wearing a floppy hat and sunglasses and clearly knew where the camera was. There was no clear shot of his face.

He paid for the gas with a credit card that turned out to be a gift card. The card was purchased at a mom-and-pop variety store without video surveillance.

So that was that. We found him, but he got away.

Chapter 56:

A few nights later Maggie and I were back in Connecticut, sitting in my kitchen, having dinner. I could tell something was bothering her.

"What's wrong?"

"I don't understand why he sold the boat."

"Because he knew he was about to be identified as a murderer. It was going to become a lot harder for him to do a complicated transaction."

"I guess. But at that point all we knew was that Emile Coulon killed two people. We didn't know anything about him owning a boat or his new name. In fact, if we didn't know about the boat, we'd have never known he was going by Martin Emmett."

"You're right. At that point we'd only just realized he was still alive. We hadn't started looking for his boat yet."

"So why did he sell it?"

"Maybe the boat was holding him back."

"Why would a boat hold him back? From the Gulf he could go to Mexico, Central America or any number of countries in the Caribbean. The boat gave him the perfect getaway vehicle."

I smiled at her.

"What?"

"Not that boat."

"Why not? It's plenty big."

"It's big, but it doesn't have a cabin. It's meant for fishing, not for living or even sleeping in."

"What are you saying?"

"Maybe we need to start visiting marinas again. What if he bought another boat? Something with a cabin. A place he could live in, sleep in, hide in and get away in."

Maggie laughed. "There's got to be a better way."

Chapter 57:

After another uneventful week in Connecticut, Maggie and I flew back to Chicago. She had to work from her office for a while, but I refused to let her be alone, not with Coulon still on the loose.

Our flight got in at 9pm and we took a cab from O'Hare to her apartment. In all the time we'd spent together, I'd never been there.

When we pulled up to her building, I was astonished. It was a towering, glass skyscraper in one of the best neighborhoods on Lakeshore Drive. Before our cab was fully stopped, a doorman was approaching. As he helped Maggie from the cab, another was hurrying to the trunk to get our luggage.

I paid the cabbie and followed Maggie and the doormen up gleaming white marble steps into the lobby. It was a spectacular combination of more white marble, glass and steel. A third doorman stepped from behind the reception desk and welcomed Maggie back. He led us to the elevator. The doorman with our bags disappeared down a hallway.

Maggie and I stepped inside. She pushed the button numbered fifty-three then put her right index finger on a fingerprint scanner.

I just stared at her as the elevator started upward.

If the building was a surprise, her apartment was a shock. The elevator doors opened into her entryway. I literally gasped. The far wall of her vast living room was what looked like a single sheet of twelve foot high, floor to ceiling glass overlooking Chicago's mostly black and white night skyline. The effect was incredible.

As we stepped from the elevator, lights came on and I saw what was inside. The main room was an open living room and dining area with a full kitchen. The floor to ceiling windows extended beyond the initial view, around an apparently seamless glass corner with views to the east over the dark lake.

I looked around, slowly turning. The inside was equally amazing. The furniture and the artwork and the appointments were all ultra-modern and sleek, but somehow subtle too. I looked from the living room to the dining area, to the kitchen, to the views, to the art on the walls. Finally, my eyes turned back to Maggie.

I stared at her, trying to understand.

A buzzer sounded in the kitchen area. She opened a door and the doorman came in with our bags. She spoke to him for a moment and then came back into the living room.

"Who are you?"

Maggie smiled and pointed toward a hallway. "Your room is back here."

"When I think of all the flea-traps we stayed in from Maine to Florida. And of the dump my house is."

"Shut up. I love your house and those flea-traps too."

"My God, Maggie. This place is incredible. Seriously, who do you work for?"

"Not now."

She showed me to my bedroom.

"I'm exhausted. Help yourself to anything you want."

She gave me a tired smile and walked down the hall.

I slept for a few hours but woke up at 4:20. I couldn't stop thinking about Coulon, how he was always a step ahead of us, watching our every move. After tossing and turning for an hour I gave up and went out to the living room. The sun was just coming up over the lake and the city opened before me. I grabbed a grapefruit Pellegrino from the fridge and sat on a couch staring out.

After a few minutes I heard the sound of Maggie's bare feet padding down the hallway. She grabbed a blanket and joined me on the white suede couch. We sat there together staring out, sharing the silence.

Chapter 58:

An hour or two later I woke up. Maggie was still on the couch, her head on the opposite arm rest.

"Morning."

"Morning."

I looked around her apartment then back out the wall of windows.

The cityscape to the south was no less beautiful and the morning sun was reflecting over the endless waters of Lake Michigan. It was breathtaking.

"Seriously, Maggie. Who are you?"

For once she didn't just smile and ignore my question. With her head still on the arm rest and both of us looking out, she said, "I'm with Richmond Sills."

Richmond Sills was a privately owned, highly respected consulting firm reputed to advise top brass from Fortune Fifty corporations and governments, both foreign and domestic.

"What do you do there?"

"I'm the strategist."

"*The* strategist? Like, the chief strategist?"

"Yes."

Her apartment was starting to make sense to me.

"Are you a partner?"

Richmond was famous for being extremely secretive about everything they did, internally and externally. Aside from some key clients, few people outside of the firm knew who the partners were or what their roles were.

"I have been, for a few years now."

She gave me a direct look. She was trusting me with extremely privileged information. I smiled, acknowledging that I understood.

"We're a private partnership. We advise public entities,

corporations, universities, business leaders, even world leaders. Our clients pay us top dollar for our advice. They are subject to public scrutiny, but that's their choice. We're private and we choose to stay that way."

Over the years Richmond Sills had received a lot of negative press about their close ties and perceived backroom dealings with business and political leaders. Maggie seemed to read my thoughts and added, "I've broken more laws working with you in the last twelve months than I have working at my firm for fifteen years. I've never broken a single law there. Not one."

I thought about our joint decision to hack into the Boston Whaler warranty website.

I moved over to her and hugged her.

"You're amazing."

She hugged me back.

Chapter 59:

While Maggie took a shower, I went to the kitchen to make breakfast. Her fridge was a little better supplied than mine.

She came out forty minutes later, dressed for work. We'd made breakfast together in my house many times and were both quiet in the morning.

She smiled and stood beside me, pouring herself a cup of coffee. I sipped my cup and poked at the sizzling bacon. Being with her felt comfortable and familiar.

"Smells good."

"It'll be ready in a few minutes."

We stood together as I cooked our bacon and eggs. Finally, I spoke. "I can't find anything. You're going to have to set the table."

She laughed and set two place settings at the kitchen table, facing out toward the lake.

We sat and started to eat.

I took a piece of toast in my hand and gestured toward the view. "This isn't bad."

"Shut up."

We took our time eating, reading the news and listening to CNN in the background. By the time we finished it was almost 10am.

"I have to go to work. I should have been there hours ago."

"Okay, but I'm going with you."

"Why?"

"Because I'm not going to leave you alone until Coulon is behind bars."

"Phil, you can't come to work with me."

"Is your office safe? Is there real security?"

"Yes. Because of the nature of what we do and the secrecy that's often involved, it's very secure. I'll be safe."

"Great. Then I'll just take you to work and bring you home."

"Don't you think you're being a little paranoid?"

"Don't you remember how we met?"

"Point taken. But I can have my firm take care of getting me to and from work. We have companies we use for security, mostly for our clients, but sometimes for us too."

"Are you sure you can trust them?"

"Yes. We deal with things like this a lot, for political figures and diplomats."

"Okay, but you have to promise me you'll take this seriously. If you want, I'll go with you to your office this morning."

"That's alright. I'll take care of it." She paused then asked, "What are you going to do while I'm at work?"

"This place seems fairly comfortable. Could I hang out here? Do you have Wifi?"

She laughed and picked up her phone and put it on speaker.

"Hello Ms. Shoshanna. This is Donald at the front desk."

"Hi Donald. I'll be coming down in twenty minutes with Mr. Philip Osgood. He's going to be staying with me for a while and I'd like to set him up with full access to my apartment and car. Including his fingerprint scan for the elevator. Could you have someone there to help set it up, please?"

"Yes, ma'am, of course."

Chapter 60:

Maggie and I were taking things lightly on the surface, but we both knew Coulon was out there. He'd killed twice and there was no reason to think he wouldn't do it again.

He'd almost gotten away with murder. If my friend Andy hadn't updated his septic system, no one would have discovered the bodies. That was just bad luck. But then I made it personal, trying to track down whoever had killed them. For Emile, everything was personal, always. I learned that lesson well. That was his mistake. If he hadn't shot me, Maggie would have never become involved, and we'd have never discovered the changed dental records. Everyone would have thought he was dead and buried with Bev. He'd have been able to live his life as Martin Emmett, free as a bird.

But he didn't leave well enough alone. He couldn't. He had to win. He had to beat me.

We'd forced him to abandon his carefully established alias, sell his dream boat and start all over again. Because of us, every policeman in the country was looking for him. His picture was everywhere. Because of us, he'd spend every minute of the rest of his life looking over his shoulder.

If he'd wanted to kill me before we'd outed him, he must have wanted to obliterate me afterwards. And Maggie too. He saw her at Hayden's office. He knew she was the one who'd figured out that he was still alive.

Even with all of that, with the authorities after him, he was in a much better position than we were. He knew exactly where to find us. We had no idea where he was. I was sure he was watching our every move, waiting for his chance to get even.

Chapter 61:

A year later there was still no sign of him.

For the first months after we lost Emile's trail in Texas, Maggie and I took the threat of him coming after us very seriously. For about a month, I lived with her. But once it was clear that her firm's security was world class, I decided to give her some space and headed back to Connecticut.

After living in Maggie's incredible apartment for an extended period, I decided to up my game. I gave up my rental and bought the third floor of a three-story walkup in the West Village, on Bank Street near Waverly. I'd always loved Manhattan and was thrilled with my new neighborhood. But I was still cautious. I stayed in my apartment as much as I could and when I did go out, I tried not to go to the same markets or restaurants. I was always alert, looking for him in crowds or store windows, sure he was there. For months I lived like a hermit, in part because I was begging Maggie to as well. Every time I went out for something frivolous or even a breath of fresh air, I felt as if I was betraying her. I couldn't expect her to do something I couldn't.

It was a lonely way to live. I missed Jenny.

I missed Maggie too, horribly. She was the only person who understood how I felt, who willingly walked down the same hard path, the only person as committed as I was to finding Emile. I felt strongly about her and knew she had strong feelings for me, but I wasn't going to allow myself the luxury of becoming involved with her. She deserved more than I could give. She wanted it all. I couldn't give her that. I loved Maggie, but my all was and would always be for Jenny.

We still spent time together every month or two, at her place in Chicago or mine in New York, and she was my closest friend, but I wouldn't let it go further.

Three of the boys worked in Manhattan and I got to see them fairly frequently, but even if I had dinner with one every week, I was usually alone for the other six nights. Most of my friends dropped me while I was suspected of being a murderer and those who remained were husbands of Jenny's friends. I lost them when I lost her.

Eventually, I couldn't take being alone. My diligence waned. I went for walks and rather than constantly going to different markets and restaurants and coffee shops, I went to the ones I liked and to convenient ones. I got sick of running on a treadmill and started to run outside, usually along the Hudson. I still worked from home, but went out for meetings with clients or brokers. My habits became more predictable. I started to live normally.

Step by step, I came out of seclusion.

Chapter 62:

One day in August eighteen months after Coulon sold his boat, I went out for an early morning run. When I got home there were seven messages on my cell and countless texts.

The first was from Scott McCallum. The second was from Emile's old Chicago landlord, Jeff Greisch. Both just said to call them, immediately.

I called Maggie first. She didn't answer.

I called Scott. His voice was weak.

"Have you heard?"

"Heard what?"

He paused, a long pause.

"What?"

"It's Maggie."

My heart broke.

Chapter 63:

Six hours later I was in Chicago.

Scott and Jeff picked me up at the airport and took me straight to Maggie's apartment building. The halfmoon driveway in front of the building was packed with marked and unmarked police cars. The front portico and lobby were teaming with cops.

I went straight up to the building. A policeman stopped me but a doorman gave him a nod and they let me into the lobby.

The head daytime doorman, Donald, was standing behind the front desk. He said something to a police detective and the detective approached me.

"Mr. Osgood?"

"Yes."

I'm Detective Gillian Pringle. I'm sorry for your loss."

I didn't respond. I couldn't.

After too brief a pause Pringle said, "I understand you had full access to Ms. Shoshanna's apartment."

I simply nodded.

"When were you last in the apartment?"

"Three weeks ago."

She gave me a skeptical look.

"I'd like you to come down to the precinct house with me to answer a few questions."

I couldn't hold back any longer. "What happened? I want to go up to her apartment."

"You can't. It's an active crime scene."

"The hell I can't."

It took several policemen to stop me.

Thirty minutes later I was sitting alone in an interrogation room in a police precinct. They left me there for another thirty. Finally Detective Pringle came in. She was with another officer.

"Mr. Osgood, this is Detective O'Malley."

I didn't acknowledge either of them.

"I'd like to ask you a few questions."

When I didn't respond she began.

"You flew in from LaGuardia this morning, on United Flight 719. Your flight left at 10:40, New York time."

It wasn't a question.

"Were you in New York last night?"

"Yes."

"Can you prove it?"

"Yes." I was snarling answers. Why was I being interrogated? We all knew who did it.

"At 7:30 last night I had dinner with my son and his wife at Sandy's on McDougal Street in Manhattan, in Greenwich Village. They know me in there. If you talk to the owner, Nina, she'll confirm it. And I bumped into a neighbor who lives on the first floor of my building, a guy named Kevin Taylor, when I got home. I think that was at about eleven."

She took down the names and addresses, expressionless.

"And I took an Uber to LaGuardia from my apartment this morning after I heard what happened."

I pulled up the payment confirmation on my phone and showed it to her. She still didn't seem satisfied.

"What was your relationship with Ms. Shoshanna?"

Her use of the past tense hit me hard.

"Look. I've had enough of this. Maggie was my best friend. And you know who killed her. If you don't, you're an idiot."

"Who killed her?"

"Oh for God sakes." I stood and started to make my way to the door.

Pringle stood. "Look Mr. Osgood, I'm aware of your background and everyone in Chicago knows who Maggie is."

"Then why are you wasting time questioning me?"

"Because last night at 2:52, you entered Ms. Shoshanna's apartment."

Chapter 64:

I was kept in custody for almost twenty hours. My best friend had been murdered and I was the prime suspect. Emile had framed me. Again.

Even after NYPD officers confirmed everything I'd said, Detective Pringle doubted my story. It was only after she saw traffic camera video footage of me crossing West Street at 12th in Manhattan at 6:07 during my morning run, just a few hours after Maggie was killed, that she finally believed I wasn't the murderer.

The rest of the world still doubted my innocence. For two days after Maggie's death, long after the police had confirmed I was in New York, papers continued to report that I, the man Maggie had saved two years earlier, was the prime suspect in her murder.

I didn't care about that. I wanted to know what had happened.

On the third morning after her death, after constant media pressure, the police commissioner held a press conference. She explained that between 2:35 and 2:45am on the night of Maggie's death, residents of her building had called the front desk complaining of cats fighting outside. Video footage showed that at 2:47 the lone late-night doorman went out the front door, presumably to try to find the source of the noise. Moments after he left, the same video showed a man in a black hoody entering the lobby. Police reported that the man used my fingerprint to access the elevator and Maggie's apartment. They speculated that the killer had somehow obtained my fingerprint and made a tactile copy that he used in the elevator. Twenty minutes later, at 3:07 the same hooded man was pictured exiting the elevator in the building's underground parking garage. By that time the doorman was back at his post. A motion detector alerted him and he watched the stranger leave on a closed-circuit monitor but had no reason to suspect anything untoward.

Maggie's body was discovered the next morning by her cleaning lady. After questioning the night doorman and watching video footage of the man in the black hoodie, police found a remote-controlled speaker hidden in the shrubs near the spot where the "cat fight" had been heard. They speculated that the killer had planted the device and played it to draw the doorman from the building.

Finally, the commissioner said that Maggie's body had been found outside her bedroom. The elevator or some other noise must have woken her. There were signs of a struggle. She was killed by several knife wounds, including one to her heart.

Chapter 65:

Three days later the coroner released her body and Maggie was buried.

In spite of all Maggie and I had been through together, I'd never met her parents. They lived in Arizona during the winter, so even when I lived at Maggie's apartment for a month, our paths hadn't crossed.

The funeral was private. I was unsure as to whether her parents wanted me to attend. I loved Maggie and wanted to be there, but I didn't want to do anything to hurt them – anything more than I'd already done.

Two nights before the funeral my cellphone rang. It was a number I didn't know.

"Hello?"

"Is this Philip Osgood?"

I felt sure it was a reporter and almost hung up.

"Yes."

"Phil, this is Matt Shoshanna, Maggie's dad."

My heart broke again.

Somehow, I managed to respond, "Hello, sir. I'm so sorry."

He cut me off. "My wife Peggy and I, we want you to come to Margaret's funeral."

I hoped he couldn't hear me crying.

The funeral was at her parents' synagogue. From what Maggie had told me I knew that none of the Shoshanna's were particularly religious, but I think having a ceremony there gave them some sense of familiarity and comfort, to the extent that was possible. Traditionally, a Jewish funeral occurs within twenty-four hours of the time of death, as a sign of respect for the deceased. Coulon took that away from Maggie too.

The Shoshannas lived in Kenilworth, just south of Winnetka where Emile had run his Chicago extortions. I got to the synagogue forty-five minutes before the funeral was scheduled to start. The quiet residential street was crowded with reporters, TV trucks, curious gawkers and the police.

As my Uber driver approached the synagogue, a policeman stopped us. A woman dressed in a black business suit carrying a clipboard approached the driver's window. I moved over to that side and powered down the rear window. She smiled an appropriately somber smile and asked for my name and some form of identification. She nodded to the cop and he waved us forward.

The massive synagogue was already three quarters full. I sat toward the back. I said a quiet prayer and teared up. I still couldn't believe Maggie was gone. I tried to compose myself and looked around. The front two rows were empty, reserved for the Shoshanna's and their closest friends.

After a moment a man who must have worked for the funeral home gently tapped my shoulder. He bent to me and whispered, "Are you Mr. Osgood?"

I nodded.

"Please follow me."

I stood, unsure of what was going to happen next. He led me to the front of the temple and stopped by the second row. Tearing up again I looked down and slid in.

Five minutes later some other people entered my row. It was Jenny and the boys and our two daughters-in-law. Jenny took my hand. "Mr. Shoshanna called me. He asked that we all come, for your sake."

To this day, the extent to which they thought of me when grieving for their own daughter humbles me. It was beyond a kindness. I tried to smile my thanks, to look at my family, but couldn't look up.

Finally, Mr. and Mrs. Shoshanna and their relatives came in. Her parents, who were about my age, greeted a few people, then turned toward me. I could see Maggie in both of their faces. She was their only child. I started to cry. We shook hands over the pew, then hugged.

Chapter 66:

In spite of how kind Maggie's parents had been and how caring Jenny and the boys had been, I left the funeral and a quiet gathering at the Shoshanna house afterwards with a deep guilt. Her own death was the price Maggie paid for helping me. Her loss was the price I paid. A hell of a price, but nothing compared to hers. My guilt distilled something in me. It crystallized my fury and the hunt into sharp clarity.

At every point, Emile had made it easy for me to walk away. From his disappearance to the bodies in Canada. Because I was hunting him, wrecking his carefully planned life, he was now destroying mine. We were agents of each others' downfalls. And since we were both in freefall, the only question was, which one of us would hit the ground first.

Police had been able to track the speaker the killer had used to play the sounds of the cat fight to a Best Buy in Chicago. Video footage showed the man who purchased the device, but he had a full beard and was wearing sunglasses and a hat. The physical profile looked like Emile, but it wasn't conclusively him. Not that that mattered. He'd killed her.

Beyond that, there was no trace of him. He must have been staying in Chicago for a while, to plan how to get into her apartment, but the police couldn't prove it. None of that mattered. Emile was done with Chicago. He only had one target left. Me.

Chapter 67:

Coulon was in a much stronger position than I was. He knew where I lived and, in a city as big as New York, could easily blend in with the crowd and watch me. He could learn my patterns and pick his spot. He didn't have to hurry. But I did wonder what he was waiting for. Every time I stepped from my apartment, I knew he might be out there watching me. Some days I was sure he was. But I wasn't afraid. I was seething. I was going to find the fucker.

The one advantage I did have was that I knew how he worked, how he watched people. He taught me to do things his way. If I could think the way he did, be like him, maybe I'd live.

I slowly developed a plan. It was complicated and expensive, but it was all I had.

My building at 26 Bank Street was a small three-story brownstone. There was one apartment on each floor and another smaller one in the basement along with a utility room. In the back, the basement opened to a small patio and garden. We all had access to the courtyard through an exit in the utility room.

Any thrill my neighbors might have felt from talking to the NYPD in the aftermath of Maggie's murder wore off in the subsequent weeks, as reporters and camera crews living outside our building relentlessly hounded them. I decided to play off that.

I told them I wanted to rebuild the back wall of our courtyard. While the side walls were the same red brick as our building, the back wall was a thatched mess. It was an eyesore. We all owned our floors and any capital improvements to the building itself had to be done with unanimous consent. To circumvent debate on the issue, I said that, to make up for what the press had put them through, I would pay for the wall. They were amenable.

Unfortunately, that only got me part way to my objective. I also had to get the approval of the owner of the building that backed up to ours and shared the back wall.

That building, 262 ½ West 12th Street, was a brownstone with only two tenants. One, who owned the entire building, lived on the three above-ground floors. The other rented the building's small basement/garden apartment. Both could access their back courtyard through a basement utility-room exit similar to ours and the owner also had access through massive glass French doors that opened from his living room to a patio and curved stone steps that led down to the courtyard.

I didn't dare even walk on West 12th Street. I couldn't risk letting Coulon see me there, if he was watching. I hired a private detective to investigate the tenants. It was the detective who learned that the man who lived on the above-ground floors owned the building. Like many people who could afford entire brownstones in Manhattan, the building was just one of his several homes. From what I had observed as his back-yard neighbor, he didn't spend much time at 262 ½.

I hired a lawyer to approach him about rebuilding our shared back wall. She offered him the same terms I offered the people in my building. Once he learned I'd pay for the wall and that the construction materials and workers would come and go through my building, he agreed.

The next part was trickier. The private detective learned that the tenant who rented the basement apartment was a graduate student at NYU studying French literature. He didn't have a police record or any obvious vices, but he was broke and swamped in debt from student loans.

I needed him to give me a key to 262 ½'s basement entrance. The key would give me access to the hallway outside his apartment and to his courtyard. It would allow me to enter and exit my apartment from the back – without being seen by anyone watching my street.

My private detective approached him at NYU and explained the request. He offered him two months' rent for his troubles. We settled on four.

My next step was to find a vantage point.

I was pretty sure that if Emile was watching me, he was probably doing it from somewhere near the corner of my street, Bank Street and the cross street, Waverly Place. My building was closer to the Waverly end of the block and the sightlines were much better from that direction.

I needed a way to watch him watch me.

Most of the buildings on my street were three- or four-story townhouses. But across the street from my townhouse, just past Waverley, there was one eight-story apartment building. All of its north- or west-facing apartments overlooked the corner of Waverly and Bank, where I thought Emile would be.

The main entrance was on Waverly, but there was a basement parking garage on the backside of the building. If I could get an apartment in that building with a north- or west-facing view, I could watch for Coulon and use the basement garage entrance to come and go from somewhere other than Bank or Waverly, so that he'd be less likely to see me.

After striking out with realtors I was able to find an eighth-floor apartment in the building through Airbnb. I had my private detective visit the apartment and take videos of the views from its windows. The vantage point was perfect. It overlooked the southeast corner of Waverly and Bank, and I could even see my building. I rented it for two months.

Two days later I had a contractor meet me at my building. I buzzed him in and we went out back and discussed the back-wall project. I had him cut an opening in the thatched back

wall so that we could see what we were dealing with from both
sides. He spent some time taking measurements and told me
he'd get me an estimate within a day or two. He offered to re-
attach the cut out, but I told him just to lean it there, because I
had two more contractors coming to bid on the project.

That afternoon I went out for a run. I made my way west
then ran north along the river. I knew I was tempting fate every time I went outside, but I wanted to bait Emile, to have
him out there, looking for me. After I finished my run, I did
some grocery shopping on Eighth Avenue then headed home,
walking right past Waverly. I showered and changed. Then I
put on a brown wig, a beard and a moustache. I felt ridiculous. I put on sunglasses and a new black Nike baseball cap.
They didn't help.

I looked out back. There wasn't anyone in the courtyard
and didn't appear to be anyone in the townhouse floors of
262 ½. I went into the back courtyard and through the new
opening in the back wall, through the basement of 262 ½ and
out onto West 12th Street. My plan had been to go straight to
the Airbnb but I decided to go for a walk first, to see if my disguise held up.

I passed a few people on 12th. No one stopped and laughed,
but I had to be sure. I'd invested too much time and money to
ruin everything by being obvious about my disguise. I walked
over to a coffee shop on Bleecker where I was a regular. I ordered a black coffee from a woman I sort of knew. She didn't
recognize me. I sat at one of the tables. No one seemed to even
notice me. I was just another guy.

Thirty minutes later I entered the garage entrance of the
Airbnb.

The apartment was perfect. The windows on the north-
west corners gave me a great view of the intersection of Bank
and Waverly and from my eighth-floor perch I was floors above

any of the other buildings in the neighborhood. I could watch Bank Street and my building but no one would be able to see me.

I was ready to implement my plan.

I tried to lure him out. Every day I'd leave my real home on Bank Street through the front door two or three times. Typically, I'd go out in the morning for coffee and errands, in the early afternoon for a run and some evenings, I'd go out for dinner.

When it appeared I was home, I'd put on my disguise, sneak out the back and hide in my Airbnb, watching for Emile.

Nine days later there was no sign of him.

Chapter 68:

On a Tuesday during the second week, I pretended to skip my run and went to the Airbnb. After three uneventful hours I decided to head to 262 ½ and home.

I got into the elevator on the eighth floor and pushed the button for the basement parking garage.

The elevator stopped on seven. Two attractive young mothers with infants in strollers backed in. I smiled and moved to the back right corner, to give them room. One of the women pushed the button for the lobby.

The elevator stopped again on five. A man got in. He looked at the women and smiled. His eyes were a deep blue, they gleamed when he smiled. He glanced at me.

It was him.

He faced forward and reached his right hand toward the panel. He reached for the basement button. He saw that it was lit and pulled his hand back. Too quickly.

We'd both rented space on the same block, in the same building. We both entered and exited through the basement so we couldn't be seen. I found him once, through his boat, and I found him again, this time by playing things the way he would. I beat him at his own game.

I watched his right hand. It was tensing.

As we passed the third floor he reached into his jacket pocket. I glimpsed the handle of a gun. I'd found him, but it wasn't over.

His fingers closed around the gun. There was a mother and a child between us. I watched the muscles in his wrist tensing as he squeezed the handle.

We passed the second floor. The elevator slowed then stopped on the ground floor.

He waited for just a moment as the door opened, until the gap was wide. I knew he was going to make his move.

As he took his first step out I pushed one of the mothers and her child to our left and lunged forward, at him. She screamed. He turned to his right and pulled his gun. The other woman screamed. He raised the gun and fired. I saw his muzzle flash and felt a bullet pierce my shoulder.

I started to go down. He smiled.

Finally, I understood what he'd been waiting for. He wanted to look me in the eye when he killed me. To show me he'd won.

He raised his gun again, aiming right at my face. He took his time, savoring the moment, his moment. His index finger contracted and curled around the trigger. Just as he was about to fire, a man from the lobby lunged at him, from his left. He turned towards the man and fired. A doorman rushed forward from the other side. Emile fired again and ran for the door.

I didn't feel any pain, only a rush of adrenalin. I flung myself up and sprinted out the door, after him. He was on the sidewalk, running. I was only ten feet behind. He looked back over his shoulder and fired.

He missed.

People dove for cover.

I got closer, only five feet behind him. He turned and faced me. The gap between us was three feet, then two. He raised his arm, taking aim. I was on him. I tackled him, driving him down onto the sidewalk. Another bullet pierced my chest.

Chapter 69:

I woke up. Everything was foggy. I was in a hospital room. I thought I saw the boys and Jenny. I looked for Maggie.

I woke up again hours or days later.

This time things were clearer. Jenny was there. She stood over me and smiled her gorgeous smile. She leaned in close and kissed me for a long, intimate moment. She broke the kiss and backed off just a bit, her face still just inches from mine.

She whispered, "Hello, Copernicus."

I tried to speak but couldn't. She saw the question in my eyes.

She smiled another smile, this time a satisfied smile.

"You did it. You found the fucker."

About the Author

Steve Powell is a retired bond trader. He's an avid runner and a struggling but optimistic golfer. Steve is married with four grown sons and lives in Connecticut.

His first book, *Charlie*, was based in small part on the still-unsolved murder of a distant relative. *Term Limits* was written in response to the US Congress' complete and ongoing ineptitude. *Stupid* is entirely a work of fiction, but was written with the real Emile in mind. Hopefully he would have gotten a kick out of his role here.

To contact Steve or order his books, visit his website:
stevepowellbooks.com

www.ingramcontent.com/pod-product-compliance
Lightning Source LLC
Jackson TN
JSHW020055100625
85842JS00008B/58

* 9 7 8 1 9 1 0 4 6 1 8 6 0 *